TOM SWIFT AND HIS
TALKING PICTURES

TOM SWIFT AND HIS TALKING PICTURES

or

The Greatest Invention on Record

by

VICTOR APPLETON

AUTHOR OF
"TOM SWIFT AND HIS OCEAN AIRPORT"
"TOM SWIFT AND HIS SKY TRAIN"
"TOM SWIFT AND HIS TELEVISION DETECTOR"

WHITMAN PUBLISHING CO.
Racine, Wis.   Poughkeepsie, N. Y.

CONTENTS

CONTENTS

TOM SWIFT AND HIS TALKING PICTURES

CHAPTER I

BLASTING FIRE

ENTERING Tom Swift's private laboratory from a room farther down the hall, Ned Newton, who seemed somewhat out of breath, glanced at the young inventor and asked:

"Do you seem to be getting anywhere with it, Tom?"

For a moment there was no reply. Tom, who had been leaning over a complicated apparatus of wires, switches, and radio bulbs that glowed dimly, was slowly turning a dial. Ned repeated his question, adding:

"What seems to be the trouble?"

"Trouble?" queried Tom, looking at Ned with eyes, however, that did not see him.

"There must be some trouble," insisted Ned, "or you'd have been capering around here on one leg when I came in after doing my stuff back

1

there," and he nodded toward the room farther down the hall. "How about it?"

Tom Swift glanced away from the apparatus, which very much resembled a radio receiving set, to a yard-square burnished sheet of metal hanging in front of him and connected to the other mechanism by several wires. This burnished sheet appeared to be made of a mirror of some metal with a square of heavy plate glass covering it.

"Can't you answer?" inquired Ned, with a chuckle. "Boy, I certainly did some acting back there all by myself! And I'd like to know whether I got it through to you. Did I? Bet I did that song and dance for the fiftieth time just now. Come on—wake up—did it come through? What's the matter, anyhow?"

"I—I'm thinking," said Tom slowly.

"Don't need an interpreter to tell me that!" and again Ned chuckled. "I can see it with half an eye. But was it a success?"

"Yes, and no," replied Tom, turning a switch which seemed to cut off some electrical current, for at once a faint hum that had been audible in the laboratory ceased. "Yes, and no. It came through all right; that is, part of it did, but the rest——"

Tom ceased speaking and bent over his apparatus. He adjusted some set screws, turned a couple of dials, and changed three of the radio tubes which, now that the power was cut off, no longer glowed with light beneath the quicksilver coatings on the thin glass.

"Do you want me to go back there and do it over?" asked Ned. "I'm willing, if you say so," and he started for the room he had just left— a room wherein, under the focused rays of a battery of powerful lights and close to a box containing a strange assortment of tubes and transmitters, Ned had done his "stunt," which consisted of singing and dancing about on a small stage. He performed alone—there was no audience but the distant one of Tom Swift in his laboratory several hundred feet away.

"Wait a minute, Ned!" Tom Swift called sharply, when his chum, who was also the financial manager of the Swift Construction Company, was about to leave the room. "I guess we might as well call it a day's work and quit."

"A night's work, you mean!" retorted Ned, pointing to the window which reflected the darkness outside. "Must be past twelve."

"I guess it is," admitted the young inventor, somewhat wearily. "I didn't notice. It's a shame to keep you at it so long, Ned."

"Oh, I don't mind!" said the other quickly. "Not as long as it's going to be a success. But is it?"

Tom Swift hesitated, looked at the complicated machine in front of him and slowly shook his head.

"Frankly, Ned, I can't say," he admitted. "You came through in a measure. Of course I heard you plainly enough over the radio—that part is simple enough. But the picture of you was too shadowy to be satisfactory. It's coming, though. I'll make it come!" and Tom, in spite of his weariness, showed some fighting spirit in his voice and manner.

"Could you identify me there?" and Ned pointed to that burnished metal mirror with its covering of glass in the lower edge of which were fused several wires.

"Oh, yes, I knew it was you, Ned, of course. But, as I say, the projected picture was too visionary. It didn't stand out clearly and with depth the way I want it to. It was like a moving picture when the man up in the booth goes to sleep on the job and the projector gets out of focus. I'm rather disappointed."

"I don't mind going back and going through my stunt again, even for the fifty-first performance," offered Ned, with enthusiasm. "I don't care how late it is. Helen won't expect me now."

"Did you have an engagement?" asked Tom, looking sharply at his friend. "And I kept you here doing a song and dance act half the night when Helen expected you! That's too bad! If I'd known——"

"Keep your hair on!" chuckled Ned. "I didn't *really* have a date with Helen. I said I might drop around if there wasn't anything to do here. But she knows you well enough to make allowances for emergency work—and this was just that."

"Yes, it is an emergency all right," returned Tom slowly. "But I shall give it up for the night. No use keeping you any longer, Ned. Go on home and I'll try it again to-morrow with a different wave length. I think that's where the difficulty is. We'll tackle it again in the morning."

"All right," assented Ned Newton, and he could not keep out of his voice a little note of satisfaction and relief. Truth to tell, he was a bit tired. For several weeks now he had been helping Tom Swift on the latter's newest idea— an invention, Tom declared, that would be the greatest on record and one that would tend to revolutionize the radio and moving picture industries.

This was a daring plan Tom had conceived of making a radio machine, both sending and receiving, that would enable a person or any number of persons not only to hear a distant per-

formance in their own home, but also see those
taking part.

"I'll make it possible," declared Tom Swift,
"for a man to sit in his easy chair, smoking a
cigar in his library, and, by a turn of a switch,
not only to hear the latest opera but also to see
each and every performer and witness the whole
play."

When Ned had asked how the vision would
appear to the man, Tom had replied:

"On an electrified screen attached to his radio
receiver by which he listens to the songs and
music."

As Tom said, the problem of transmitting an
entire opera through the air was simple enough.
That had been done many times. So had the
transmitting of photographs by wireless. Also,
in a limited way, television had made it possible
for a person in a dark room to be visible to
lookers-on in another apartment some distance
away.

"But I am going to combine the two!" declared Tom Swift. "I want to make it possible
for a synchronized performance of seeing and
hearing to take place. Thus when a theater is
equipped with my sending apparatus and I have
perfected my receiver, one need never go outside
the house to enjoy a theatrical performance or a
concert."

"But even if you're successful, you won't make any money out of it," declared Ned Newton, after first hearing of his chum's ambitions. "Look at the radio people! The air is free. Anybody who wants to can tune in and listen to a million dollar concert without paying a cent. They don't even have to buy any special kind of receiver—they can roll their own, so to speak. What's to prevent them from stealing your stuff —your—what do you call it, anyhow?"

"I haven't settled on a name," Tom said, with a smile. "Call it talking pictures for the time being. Of course it's entirely different from moving pictures with phonograph attachment."

"Well, what's to prevent any one from tuning in on your talking pictures?" asked Ned.

"This," answered Tom, pointing to a small tube on one side of the receiving apparatus. "This is a new device. Without it no one can see and hear my pictures that will talk. This is protected by patents and no one can use it without my sanction. That's the secret."

"Well, maybe you've got something there," Ned admitted.

So, during the past months, he had helped Tom Swift bring the new apparatus to such perfection as it now had.

The present night's performance was only one of many. At first there had been only blank failure. But by using different kinds of receiving screens, finally settling on a mirror covered with electrified glass, Tom had achieved a measure of success. Still, even now, the projected image of the singing or talking performer in a distant room was too dim to be commercially successful.

"We'll go at it again to-morrow," Tom told his chum as he let him out of the laboratory and locked the door after him.

"It's the biggest thing I ever attempted," he said to himself, when Ned had gone and he was alone in the room. "the very biggest, and I'm not going to have it stolen from me. No one suspects as yet what I am working on—no one except dad and Ned. But I wish I were nearer success. I thought the image would come through clear to-night, but there was that same haze—that same haze. I wonder——"

He paused and listened intently. Outside his door he heard footsteps—cautious footsteps.

"Is that you, Ned?" he called. "Anything wrong?"

Tom did not open the door—he was taking no chances.

"That you, Ned?" he asked again, more sharply.

"No, Mr. Swift," came back a voice with a foreign accent. "I am just leaving my own laboratory. I think I have perfected that new magnetic gear shift we have been working on."

"That's good," Tom responded. He recognized the voice of Jacob Greenbaum, a clever inventor whom he had recently engaged to work on some side lines that occupied the Swift factory. Tom had an idea for a new device to make easier the shifting of gears on automobiles. It was an adaptation of the old magnetic selection that has often been tried and which, up to date, had not been successful.

"Do you want to take a look at it?" asked Greenbaum, and from the nearness of the voice Tom knew that the man was just outside the locked door.

"No, thank you, Greenbaum, not now," the young inventor replied. "I am busy at something else. I'll see you in the morning."

"You are working late, Mr. Swift," went on the man. "Could I be of any service to you? I should be glad——"

"No, thank you," Tom said. "As for lateness, you are doing a bit of overtime yourself."

"Oh, yes; but I do not mind. I think I am on the right track. If you would take a look——"

"No, not now," and Tom's voice was a bit sharp. "I am busy. Good night!"

There was no response for a moment, and then came a short:

"Good night!"

Greenbaum, however, did not immediately move away from the door and a look of annoyance passed over Tom's face as he bent over his secret apparatus.

"What's he hanging around for?" thought Tom. "I wonder if he can be a spy? Two or three times I've caught him lurking around my private laboratory. But he can't get in since I put on the new lock, and I know he hasn't so much as poked his nose in during the times I have been here experimenting. Still, I wonder——"

He was about to call out, to tell the man to go away when footsteps were heard moving down the corridor and toward the outer door of the small shop where most of the experimental work was carried on.

"Good riddance," murmured Tom Swift. "I don't want to be unjust to a good workman, and Greenbaum is all of that, but I must confess I don't like the way he hangs around me. As soon as he finishes that magnetic gear shift I'll pay him well and let him go. Now let's see if I can think up another way of doing this. Perhaps if I hooked up the wave distributor to the vibratory selector instead of to the polarizer we'd get better vision. I'll try that and have Ned perform again to-morrow. Now I'll take a look to see that my wire connections are all right and then I think I'll go to bed. I'm tired."

Tom spent perhaps another half hour in getting things in readiness for some new experiments, and, having made sure that everything connected with his secret was put out of sight of possible prying eyes, the young inventor started toward the door.

He inspected the new combination lock he had had put on, noting that it was properly set, and then opened the door to step out. The experimental laboratory was only a short walk from Tom's home, the back of the Swift Construction plant being some distance away.

As Tom opened the door there was a click, followed at once by a blinding flash of blasting fire. Then a dull explosion shook the building. Tom had no chance to leap back. The force of the blast hurled him forward, across the corridor and out through a wire-screened window into the yard. He fell heavily, uttered an inarticulate cry, and then seemed to be sinking down into a pit of dense blackness.

CHAPTER II

NED DISAPPEARS

SCARCELY had the echoes of the explosion in Tom Swift's laboratory died away, being swallowed up in the blackness and silence of the night, than members of the Swift household began stirring.

Mr. Swift, Tom's aged and rather infirm father, sat up in bed and called:

"What was that? Thunder?"

"No, Massa Swift," answered Eradicate, the faithful colored servant, who, now that Mr. Swift had declined so, was his personal attendant, sleeping in the next room. "No, Massa Swift," he repeated. "Dat wa'n't no thunder."

By this time Eradicate was moving about and fumbling for a light. Mr. Swift, however, had reached up and switched on the reading lamp attached to the head of his bed.

"What was it then?" asked the aged inventor, for Mr. Swift had begun invention work when Tom was a mere baby.

"I spects, Massa, dat it was somethin' Tom been doin' out in his lab'tory," the colored man answered. He had his own light on now and was beginning to dress, preparatory to making an investigation.

"If Tom was in the midst of anything that made a noise like that he must be hurt!" declared Mr. Swift. "That was a sharp explosion. Hurry, Rad, and see what it was."

"Yes, sah, Massa Swift, I's a-hurryin'!" answered Eradicate.

From a room farther down the hall in the Swift home came a deep, heavy voice exclaiming:

"Fire! Fire! Koku see much blaze!"

Koku was a gigantic specimen of a man whom Tom had brought back with him from an airship trip to a distant, mysterious land. The giant was rather simple, and never seemed to be able to master the English language. But he was a faithful servant and, because of his enormous strength, Tom frequently used Koku as a guard about the plant.

"Fire?" cried Mr. Swift, fumbling for his clothes. "Is there a fire, Koku?"

"Much blaze in Master Tom's workshop," the giant replied. He could not twist his tongue around "laboratory."

"Dey suah is a fire!" cried Eradicate, running

to his window. "By golly, whole place looks like it was burnin'!"

By this time Mrs. Baggert, the housekeeper, several other servants, and Garret Jackson, the shop manager and superintendent, who was spending the night at the Swift home, had been aroused. Several workmen in the Swift plant, who lived not far from the experimental laboratory, had also been aroused by the explosion and the glare of flames and were now running to help, adding their voices to the others giving the alarm.

By this time Mr. Swift, with Eradicate and Koku, had descended to the yard that was between the laboratory and the house, and by the glare of the flames Tom's inert body was seen stretched out on the grass.

Eradicate and Koku bent over the body of the young inventor. Koku felt for the heart and found it beating.

"Master Tom no dead," said the giant simply.

"Then carry him into the house, and send for a doctor at once," directed Mr. Swift. "Oh, what could have happened? The whole place will go up in flames and Tom's valuable new invention will be destroyed!"

"Dat fire'll soon be out!" predicted Eradicate, and Koku, lifting Tom like a child, started to-

ward the house with him. "Fire not so bad,
after all, Massa Swift!"

While the injured inventor is being ministered
to I shall take a brief moment to acquaint new
readers with a few facts regarding Tom Swift.

He was a young man, well set up physically,
and in spite of the fact that he was young, had
to his credit many important inventions, not
a few of which had been adopted by the United
States Government.

Tom's mother was dead, but he and his father
were well looked after by Mrs. Baggert, the
housekeeper. As related in the first volume of
this series, entitled "Tom Swift and His Motor-
cycle," the youth began his inventive activities
early. Wakefield Damon, who lived in the
neighboring town of Waterfield, had, some years
before this present story opens, bought a motor-
cycle. Not knowing much about such machines, Mr. Damon soon found himself climbing
a tree near Tom's home.

Tom rescued the eccentric individual and,
"blessing" many animate and inanimate objects
from his rubber boots to his collar button, Mr.
Damon declared he was through with motor-
cycles. Tom bought the damaged machine, re-
paired and improved it and had several thrilling
adventures on it. From then on his inventions

followed one another and they were not yet
ended. In the volume immediately preceding
this and named "Tom Swift Circling the Globe,"
you may read of the further doings of the young
inventor.

Tom had many friends and not a few enemies,
the latter chiefly unscrupulous men who had
tried to steal his inventions but who had been
worsted by Tom, with the aid of Mr. Damon,
Ned Newton, Eradicate and Koku.

Tom always insisted that Mary Nestor, a
beautiful girl to whom the young inventor was
practically engaged, had a lot to do with his
success, but Mary always smiled tolerantly when
her friend said this.

"What do I do, Tom?" she would ask.

"You give me inspiration," he would answer,
"and that, to an inventor, is the one thing
needed."

Whether Mary Nestor was the inspiration for
Tom's latest talking picture invention does not
matter, but the fact remains that Tom was in
the midst of perfecting that machine when the
explosion occurred.

While the fire was being brought under control by several of the shop men, under the direction of Mr. Jackson, the young inventor was
hurriedly carried into his home and laid on a
bed. Mrs. Baggert, sensing that medical aid

might be needed, had, almost as soon as she got up after the alarm, telephoned for the nearest doctor. So it was not long after the explosion before Tom was in the care of the medical man.

"Is he badly hurt?" asked Mr. Swift, anxiously hovering around the room.

"I think not," was the cheerful reply of Dr. Layton. "He has had a shock and is suffering more from that than from actual injuries, though he is cut and bruised and has some nasty burns. But we will soon make him comfortable."

"He is still unconscious, though, isn't he?" asked Mr. Swift.

"Yes," Dr. Layton admitted. "But that is nothing to worry about. Nature will take care of that. It is better to let his senses come back gradually rather than to give some strong stimulant that will shock him into wakefulness and perhaps do more harm than good. I'll make him as comfortable as I can and we'll just wait for him to rouse."

The burns and cuts were dressed, Koku being of great service because he could lift and move Tom as if the young man were a baby. Yet Tom was of husky build, strong and muscular. The giant made an ideal nurse in a case like this, though Eradicate, who had a deep love for

Tom Swift, fluttered eagerly about, anxious to do something to help. Mrs. Baggert had him bring hot water and bandages, and this gave Eradicate as much pleasure as Koku found in ministering more personally to his young master.

After the first alarm over Tom's condition was over and when it was apparent that there was no immediate danger, Mr. Swift went out to see what damage had been done and if there was any further danger from the fire and explosion.

The flames, by this time, were subdued. There had been a second but slight, explosion. This, however, did little damage, as the force of it was directed toward the outer corridor, part of the wall of which was blown away. The greatest force of the first explosion, likewise, had been in the same direction, and though the door of Tom's private laboratory had been stove in and some of his valuable apparatus scattered about and burned, fortunately no great damage was done to the secret room.

Ascertaining this and knowing how jealously Tom guarded the new secret, Mr. Swift had some of the men nail the laboratory up, an improvised door being made and boards being fastened over the shattered windows.

Tom had been blown through a window in the corridor outside his laboratory. But, luckily, the window was up at the bottom, and Tom had shot through a wire mosquito screen instead of through the glass. In spite of this, and the fact that he had landed in a clump of deep, thick grass, the young inventor had not come off scatheless from the accident.

"Things aren't as bad as they seemed at first, Mr. Swift," reported Mr. Jackson a few hours after the explosion. "The fire is all out now and Tom's things don't seem to be much damaged. I've got several men on guard. They'll stay there the rest of the night."

"It will soon be morning," murmured the old gentleman. "Thank you, Jackson."

"I wonder how much longer Tom will remain unconscious?" Mr. Swift said, entering the sickroom and glancing toward the bed on which his son lay.

"I think he is coming around now," said the doctor softly, as he moved to his patient's side. "Yes, he is coming out of it," he added. "How do you feel?" he asked as Tom opened his eyes and stared about.

"Pretty—pretty—rocky," was the husky answer. "What—what happened?" he asked in a stronger voice. Then, as recollection came back to him, Tom went on: "I remember now. There was an explosion just as I was coming out of my laboratory. Is it gone? Is everything gone?" and he tried to get up. Dr. Layton pushed him back.

"Now lie still," said the doctor. "Things aren't half as bad as you think, and you're not much hurt."

"I don't care about myself!" declared Tom fiercely. "But if that new—that machine is blown up—" He looked anxiously at his father, the only other person in the room who knew about the secret of the talking-picture invention.

"It's all right, Tom," the aged inventor made haste to say. "The door and windows of your laboratory were blown out and some of your apparatus damaged by the fire and explosion. But your—the main object is all right," he finished, and Tom understood.

Before Tom could ask any more questions, Dr. Layton administered a sedative to quiet his patient's nerves, and, after a few more questions had been answered to the satisfaction of the young inventor, he sank back into a sleep.

Not before, however, he had told his father and the others that he had no idea what had caused the explosion and fire.

"Was it an electrical blast?" Mr. Swift wanted to know. He was aware that often a high tension current may act almost like a blast of dynamite.

"I think not," Tom had said. "I examined

my wires the last thing, after Greenbaum had left the building, and they were all right. The explosion seemed to be coincident with my opening of the door."

"It were a bomb! Dat's whut it were—a bomb!" declared Eradicate. "An' ef I kotches de feller whut done planted it I——"

"That will do now, Rad," whispered Mrs. Baggert. "Tom must be kept quiet."

The injured young inventor was now sleeping quietly, and Dr. Layton said he would remain until morning to see how Tom was when he awakened again. Then, the fire being out and no more danger appearing, the house became quiet.

But Mr. Swift had a worried, anxious air. He could not account for that explosion. Some more of Tom's enemies must be at work, was the conclusion of the aged inventor.

The sun was rising and Tom was just awakening again when the telephone rang. Mrs. Baggert, answering it, brought word that Mary Nestor was on the wire and wanted to know how badly Tom was hurt.

"How'd she hear about it?" Tom demanded when he was prevented from answering the call in person.

"Why, it seems," reported the housekeeper, "that the town fire-department responded to the alarm. However, they weren't needed, as your own men put out the blaze, Mr. Swift. However, it was rumored that you were hurt and Mary heard of it. What shall I tell her?"

"Tell her I'm all right and that I'll be over as soon as I can get dressed," Tom answered.

"No you won't!" chuckled Dr. Layton. "You're not badly hurt, but I'm taking no chances with you and you'll stay in bed all day. Miss Nestor can call here if she likes," he conceded, with a smile.

"Thanks for that favor," and Tom smiled in answer. "Tell her, please, Mrs. Baggert."

"I will," and the housekeeper hurried back to the telephone.

A further inspection of Tom's injuries by daylight did not reveal them as any worse than the first diagnosis indicated and Dr. Layton said that his patient would be up and about in a few days.

"And when I am things are going to hum!" declared Tom.

He had finished a light breakfast and the medical man was preparing to depart when the telephone rang again.

"If that's Mary I'm going to speak to her!" exclaimed Tom.

"But it isn't," said Mrs. Baggert, with a smile, coming in from the hall outside Tom's room, the telephone being installed in a booth in the corridor. "It's Mr. Newton."

"Ned?" exclaimed Tom Swift.

"No, not Ned—his father," replied the housekeeper. "He wants to know when Ned will be home."

"When Ned will be home!" exclaimed Tom, in bewildered surprise. "Why, I thought he was at home now. He left me before midnight to go home."

"He isn't there," said Mrs. Baggert. "Mr. Newton says Ned hasn't been home all night and he thought he must be here, as he often stays all night, you know."

"Yes, I know," admitted Tom, with a puzzled look on his face. "But he didn't stay last night. He started for home. He was dead tired from helping me. Ask Mr. Newton if he is sure Ned isn't sleeping soundly in his own room."

Mrs. Baggert went back to the telephone. In a few moments she came back.

"Ned seems to have disappeared," she announced. "He didn't come home or send any word. Mr. Newton is quite worried. He wants to talk to you."

CHAPTER III

TOM SWIFT looked at Dr. Layton. The medical man had paused in his departure on hearing the telephone bell and the ensuing talk.

"Doctor," began Tom, "I don't want to disobey your advice, but I've simply got to talk to Ned's father. Something may have happened. I'm beginning to get worried. There may be more at the bottom of this than just an accidental explosion in my laboratory."

"I'd rather you stayed in bed," said the physician. "You oughtn't to move around so soon after such a shock. Can't you move the telephone in here?"

"I'll get an extension wire that I have in my room and plug it in," offered Mr. Swift, and while Mrs. Baggert was telling Mr. Newton that Tom would soon speak to him, Mr. Swift, with the help of Eradicate, quickly had an extension telephone rigged up at Tom's bedside. Then the young inventor talked to the father of his business manager.

"Are you sure, Mr. Newton, that Ned isn't in the house, sleeping his head off?" was Tom's first question.

"No, he isn't here," was the worried answer. "When he didn't come down to breakfast we didn't think anything of it at first, as he was going to be at your place late, he said, and we wanted to let him get as much rest as he could.

"But when we looked into his room a little while ago to see how he was sleeping, he wasn't there. His mother said that she hadn't heard him come in during the night, but even then we weren't alarmed. We thought he had spent the night with you, as he so often does."

"No," Tom said slowly, "Ned isn't here. He left my laboratory somewhere around midnight and I thought he was going straight home. But wait a minute!" Tom exclaimed as a new idea came to him. "I just happened to think. He might have gone to see Miss Morton and have stayed there all night, being too tired to pull up and head for home."

Ned Newton was engaged to Miss Morton and, more than once after calling there and finding himself stormbound, he had been persuaded by her parents to remain over night.

"I think you'll find him there," suggested Tom, though in his heart he remembered that Ned had said it was too late to go to see Helen.

Besides, he had had no positive engagement with her. "Call up the Mortons," was Tom's final suggestion.

"I will," agreed Mr. Newton. "Thanks."

Tom had no sooner finished his breakfast, following the departure of Dr. Layton, than the extension telephone rang again, and once more Mr. Newton was on the line.

"Ned wasn't at Helen's," the father of the mysteriously missing young man reported. "Oh, Tom, what do you think could have happened?"

The young inventor was at a loss for an answer. Rapidly he reviewed the situation in his mind. Ned had left the laboratory, he was sure of that—or, wait a moment, was he? He had not seen Ned go out, but had taken it for granted that such had occurred. Then Tom had puzzled a bit over his latest invention before starting for his house. Then had come the explosion and——

Perhaps Ned had not left the laboratory. He may have gone to one of the private rooms and turned in there. Tom kept two bedrooms in this building for the use of himself and his manager when they were working late at night and did not want to disturb the main household. That might be it. Ned might be asleep in the laboratory.

"Wait a few minutes, Mr. Newton," Tom advised over the wire. "I have just thought of something. It is barely possible that Ned didn't start for home after all last night. He isn't at our house, but he may be in the laboratory. I'll send out and have a search made. I'll call you up in a few minutes."

"All right, Tom. But what's this I've heard about a fire at your place last night?"

"Oh, there was a little blaze—it didn't amount to anything," was the reply. Tom said nothing about the explosion. He wanted to minimize the damage, and he believed what had been told him, that it really did not amount to much.

"Koku," he called to the giant, "you and Rad hurry out to my laboratory and look for Mr. Newton. He may be in one of the bedrooms, asleep."

"Asleep, Tom, after that explosion?" exclaimed Mr. Swift incredulously.

The telephone receiver had been hung back on the hook, so Mr. Newton heard none of this talk.

"It doesn't seem possible," Tom had to admit to his father; "but still I can't account for Ned's disappearance in any other way. He was dead tired and he may have slept through the fire and explosion. We'll soon find out. I wish I could go and take a look for myself."

"No, you stay here!" his father ordered. "Obey the doctor's advice. Koku and Rad will find Ned if he's to be found."

The giant and negro came back soon, to report that there was no sign of Ned in the laboratory.

"Perhaps he may have returned home by this time," suggested Mr. Swift. "Better call up and find out."

"There is just a bare possibility—" said Tom musingly, as he reached for the 'phone, "there is just a bare chance that Ned took the midnight train for New York to get the selenium."

"Took the midnight train to get selenium!" exclaimed Mr. Swift. "What do you mean?"

"Well, I needed some more sensitive selenium for my—for my—new experiment," Tom said, knowing his father would understand he was speaking of the talking picture machine. "Ned knew about it and planned to go after it to-day. When he left me last night he may have decided suddenly to keep right on to New York. I think I'll tell his father that."

"Do you really believe it, Tom?"

"No, Dad, I don't. But I don't want Mr. Newton to give up hope until I can get on the job myself and help hunt for Ned. Even at that there is a bare chance he did go to New York. I'll suggest that to his father."

Mr. Newton received this ray of hope gratefully and Tom was glad he had thought of it, though he knew it was only a shadow. If Ned really had taken the midnight train, which was possible, there ought to come a message from him soon reporting on the selenium matter. Also, Ned, being a home-loving young man, would naturally be expected to send word to his family about his return.

"It will only hold matters back for a short time at best," said Tom to his father. "But I didn't imagine my laboratory was burned enough to destroy the bedrooms. Do you think there is much more damage, Jackson?"

"Not to your laboratory," was the reassuring reply. "You see, after the explosion the flames shot up at the back before we knew it, and the draft sucked them in through the bedroom windows. So the upper part of the place was worse burned than the lower. But Ned Newton was not in there."

"I'm glad of that," Tom said.

He was beginning to feel the strain of what he had gone through, and he was glad when, a little later, Mary Nestor and her father motored over to see him.

Mr. Nestor had some time before taken a long trip North for his health, a trip that had greatly improved his condition.

"Oh, Tom, what happened?" exclaimed Mary when she saw him in bed, all bandaged up.

"That's what I'd like to know," he answered, with a smile. "It was like a premature Fourth of July celebration."

"Are you much hurt?" the girl faltered.

"Nothing more than shock and scratches," Tom answered. "I'll be up and around in another day."

However, it was three days before Dr. Layton would allow Tom to get out of bed. Meanwhile nothing had been heard from Ned Newton. He had not gone to New York, that was evident, unless something had happened to him there, and he was not around Shopton, the town on Lake Carlopa where the Swifts' large plant was located.

"It's mighty queer," said the worried Mr. Newton, when Tom was forced to admit that his New York theory was useless. "Where could he be keeping himself?"

"I can't imagine," Tom said. He was much broken up over the disappearance of his chum. He knew Ned well enough to know that he was not staying away from choice, though Tom did not communicate his suspicions to Mr. Newton.

As soon as Tom was able, he went out to the laboratory. The scene of ruin on the lower floor was not so bad as he had feared, but the back and upper part of the laboratory was pretty well burned away. Then Tom had the improvised nailed-up door removed so he might enter the room where he had set up his talking-picture machine.

"I hope it's all right," the young inventor murmured as he approached the apparatus. "They said it was, after the fire and explosion, but——"

He gave a cry of dismay as he saw that, though the main part of the marvelous new machine was intact, the force of the explosion had wrecked the delicate mechanism that he depended on to prevent any but authorized owners of the apparatus from using it. Tom's secret invention was badly damaged. In addition, all the new radio tubes, of a kind never before used, had been shattered by the blast.

"This sure is tough luck!" murmured Tom Swift. "This knocks me out! The fire wasn't so bad, but the explosion—whew! This certainly is tough! But I'll work double time and soon have it in shape again, and better than ever. Luckily, I have duplicate parts of that secret check apparatus, and I can get new tubes, though it will take time."

"You'd better go slow, Tom," advised his father, who had come into the partly wrecked private room with his son. "First thing you know, you'll blow yourself to pieces with these experiments of yours."

"It was no experiment of mine, Dad, that caused the explosion here!" said Tom decidedly.

"It wasn't?"

"No. All my wires were in good shape. It was some outside force that did the damage. I believe some one planted an infernal machine in here, Dad!"

"You do, Tom? Whom do you suspect?"

"I—I hardly know what to say," was the slow answer. "But I have one man in mind. Where's Clark?" he asked suddenly, naming a young workman who was much in Tom's confidence.

"I'll send him to you," Mr. Swift offered. "What's the matter, Tom? What are you going to have Clark do?"

"Some detective work," was the low answer.

CHAPTER IV

A STRANGE MESSAGE

Tom Swift sank wearily into a chair, facing his damaged talking-picture machine. That it was very seriously damaged was plainer to the eyes of the young inventor than to those even of his father, who was one of three persons aware of what great changes the new machine was destined to bring about. But Tom rallied and from the ruins of his invention saw mentally, rising like the fabled Phœnix from its own ashes, a new and better piece of apparatus.

"Maybe, after all," mused Tom, "this will turn out better than it looked at first sight. I already have an idea for some improvements in the new machine I'm going to start—as soon as I'm able," he added somewhat grimly.

"Tom, you'd better go back to bed!" exclaimed his father anxiously. "You know Dr. Layton said——"

"Oh, I'm all right!" protested the young inventor. "I'm going slow. I do feel a bit pulled out, but I don't intend to do any work. However, I'm on the track of something, and it's got to be followed up."

"Then you think this was deliberately done, Tom?" asked Mr. Swift as he finished sending a message to have Jim Clark sent to Tom's private quarters.

"I'm almost positive of it," was the reply. "And I have under suspicion a certain man."

"Who?" asked Mr. Swift in a low voice, making sure no one was near the shattered door.

"Greenbaum," was the equally low answer.

"Why, I thought he was one of your best workers, Tom!" exclaimed Mr. Swift in surprise.

"So he is, in his own particular line. But now that I think matters over, I see that there is a chance he had something to do with this explosion. He was here in the laboratory just before it happened. He and I and Ned Newton were the only ones here, as a matter of fact. Ned has disappeared, and that's worrying me, but I'll come to that feature in due time. I guess Ned can look after himself, though his disappearance is certainly mysterious, coupled with everything else that's happened. But when I stop to think about Greenbaum being here just before the explosion——"

"But, Tom," interrupted his father, "I

thought you said Greenbaum went before you locked up and came home."

"Apparently he did. But he may have come back. That's what I want Clark to do—a bit of detective work to find out if Greenbaum went to his boarding house and stayed there. If he did——"

The entrance, at that moment, of the young workman in whom Tom placed much confidence brought a sudden end to the talk.

"You sent for me, Mr. Swift?" asked Clark, with a smile. "Is it about the new negative gravity machine I'm working on?"

"Not this time, Clark," answered Tom, motioning the young fellow to take a chair near the scorched desk which was not far from the shattered talking-picture machine. That apparatus had, however, been covered from prying eyes. "I want you to do a bit of detective work, if you will," went on the young inventor.

Without telling just why he wanted the information, Tom instructed his agent to find out in secret something about Greenbaum, seeking to learn just what the man did on the night of the explosion.

"I get you!" exclaimed Clark, with ready wit. "I'm wise all right. I'll shadow him if you want me to."

"No, don't dog him," objected Tom. "Just

trace his movements. You can tell your fore-
man you're working for me and it will be all
right."

With Clark dispatched on this mission, Tom
took from the partial wreck of his new apparatus such pieces as were vital for rebuilding it
and then, asking his father to have the laboratory cleaned up and put in working shape again,
Tom went back to his bedroom.

Truth to tell, he was pretty well fagged out,
not so much physically as mentally. The shock
both to his hopes and his body, as well as worry
over Ned's disappearance, was beginning to tell.

"Hadn't you better give this up, Tom?" asked
his father as, having set men to putting the laboratory to rights, he went to his son's room
where he found Tom stretched out on a long
sofa.

"Give what up, Dad? You mean trying to
find out who blew me up and why Ned is missing? Give those problems up?"

"No, I mean work on this new talking-picture
machine of yours. I don't believe it will ever
work, Tom."

"But it has worked, Dad!" exclaimed the
young man, with enthusiasm. "Only about an
hour before Ned left and the explosion happened,
I got a pretty fine record of what Ned did in the
theater room," for so Tom called the apartment

with its battery of bright lights where the young manager had sung and danced.

"You heard Ned's voice?" asked Mr. Swift.

"Perfectly," declared Tom. "Saw him, too. But the vision was not as clear as it's got to be to make this a commercial success. But I know how to improve it, and I'm going to. I can't give that up, Dad!"

"It might be better if you did, Tom."

"Better? How?"

"Well, for your own safety. You're using powerful electrical currents and you've had one explosion already; so——"

"But didn't I tell you, Dad," and Tom smiled tolerantly, "that this explosion was none of my doing? Nothing went wrong with the wires. They were all in shape and I was just opening the door when something went off. It was something that was set, too—a bomb, if I guess aright."

"All the more reason for giving it up, Tom."

"What do you mean, Dad?"

"I mean that perhaps some one, or perhaps a number of persons, don't want this new invention to succeed. Think what it will mean to the moving-picture industry if you can give people in their own homes entertainment such as the big theaters present. And where will the theaters come out if their high-priced shows can be picked up by every one who buys one of your machines?"

"That's their lookout," said Tom. "It was said that the radio would kill the phonograph; and it nearly did, but the phonograph folks came back strong."

"This is different, Tom."

"Yes, I know it is—different and better. No, I'm not going to back out, bombs or no bombs! Besides, Dad, you must realize that we are in this thing pretty deep."

"Deep, Tom? What do you mean?"

"I mean we have a large amount of money tied up in this thing—more than I like to think about. I've just got to come through with it to break even."

"Well, Tom, I suppose you know best," said the aged inventor, with rather a weary smile. "But be careful of yourself."

When Mrs. Baggert had put new bandages on some of Tom's burns and he had taken a little rest, he called up Ned's home, only to learn that no word had come from him. His parents were greatly worried, for Ned was not selfish and was not the kind of young man to remain long away from home without sending word.

"He may have decided to take a little unannounced vacation," Tom told Mr. Newton, "and have gone to the country. He may have sent word and the letter or the message has failed to arrive. Shall I notify the police?"

"No, not yet," decided Mr. Newton. "Ned may be all right and he'd hate any police notoriety. We'll wait a few days."

The few days that followed were anxious ones, not only for Ned's parents, but also for Tom Swift. He had a double worry, divided between the disappearance of his trusted chum and manager and concern over the wreck of his new apparatus. The latter worry was more easily disposed of, however, though it meant hard work and delay.

Tom set some of his most trusted men at the labor of reconstructing the new apparatus, but in such a way that the secret could not be come at. Only certain unimportant parts were given out, and Tom and his father would make the more vital sections.

Since Tom already had on the market a telephoto machine and had also made several varieties of moving picture projectors, it was not a hard matter to let it casually be known that the new apparatus was an attempt to improve either or both of the old inventions. Thus was gossip stilled about the big Swift plant.

Tom, however, did not know what to think about Greenbaum. The day after the explosion the man was lamenting loudly that some of his own experimental apparatus, which he was working on for the Swift firm, had been destroyed in the fire and blast.

"And," said Tom, telling his father about it, "since I have promised him a large bonus if he works out that magnetic gear shift, it doesn't seem reasonable that he would set a bomb that might destroy the results of his own hard work."

"No, Tom, it doesn't."

"And yet I can't help suspecting him," mused the young inventor. "He is as friendly as ever, and seems anxious to help me. But there is something furtive in his manner and in his looks."

"Did Clark find out anything?"

"Only that Greenbaum went straight to his boarding place from here and did not go out again that night. He was at home when the explosion took place."

"Then that clears him, Tom."

"No, Dad, it doesn't. He could easily have planted a time bomb or rigged one up that was operated when I opened the door. I shall still suspect him. But I've got something else to do now."

"What is that?"

"I want to see how Jackson is coming on with the new radio tubes he is making for the talking-picture machine and I've got to do something about Ned. His unexplained absence for so long a time is getting serious now. It doesn't seem possible that he is remaining away voluntarily without sending some word."

"No, Tom, it doesn't. What do you think?" and Mr. Swift looked up from his work. He was making some delicate tests with a galvanometer in the laboratory, which had been cleaned out and temporarily fitted up to be used again.

"I'm thinking, Dad, that perhaps Ned, in some way, was concerned with the fire and explosion."

"Tom! You don't mean that Ned——"

"Oh, of course I don't mean that he set it, Dad!" and Tom laughed at his father's shocked face. "I mean that the same rascals who tried to blow me up kidnapped Ned."

"Kidnapped a young man like Ned Newton! A strong, husky chap——"

"They may have caught him napping," said Tom. "Anyhow, I've got to do something. Ned's folks are much worried."

"Why don't you go to the police?"

"I think a private detective would be better. Or, best of all, I'll get Clark and set out on the trail myself. I've got things begun on the rebuilding of my new machine now, and I've really got to do something about Ned."

"I agree with you, Tom. I was just wondering——"

What he wondered Mr. Swift never stated, as at that moment a voice was heard out in the corridor, saying:

"Bless my storage battery, you needn't show me the way in, Eradicate! I guess I can find Tom Swift, or what's left of him! My! My! It must have been terrible! Bless my stick of dynamite! So they tried to blow Tom up!"

"It's Mr. Damon!" said Mr. Swift, smiling at his son.

"No need for him to send in a card!" chuckled the young inventor. "His voice and talk give him away. Come in, Mr. Damon!" he called, and the door opened to give entrance to the eccentric, kindly old gentleman who, indirectly, had been the means of Tom's starting on his great inventive career.

"Bless my handkerchief, Tom!" exclaimed Mr. Damon, vigorously mopping his face with the linen article in question, while he held out one hand to the young inventor. "What's all this I hear about you? I just got back from a Western trip and my wife tells me you were blown sky high, that your plant was demolished, and that the whole business is in ruins. Bless my insurance policies! Whew!"

"Not quite so bad as that," Tom answered, with a laugh.

"But something happened, bless my thermometer if it didn't!" declared Mr. Damon, pointing to a bandage on Tom's left hand.

"Yes, there was an accident," and in a few words Tom told what had happened, without, however, making mention of the new machine, which was too deep a secret as yet for even so close a friend as the eccentric man to share. "But it might have been worse," concluded the young man. "And, as a matter of fact, that isn't the worst that's happened."

"No, Tom? What else? Bless my spectacles!"

"Ned Newton has mysteriously vanished," said Tom, with a serious face, and he told as much as he knew about the strange occurrence.

"That's terrible!" declared Mr. Damon. "It's the worst outrage I ever heard of! But I came back just in time, Tom Swift."

"Time for what?"

"To help you hunt for Ned! Now, don't stop me! I'm going to do it. I'll devote all my time and half my fortune to finding my young friend and your chum. Tell me more about it."

"I've told you all I know, which isn't much,"

Tom answered. "But suppose we go to the house. I'm about through here," and he looked around the laboratory, asking his father to close and lock it when he left. "We'll go over to the house, Mr. Damon."

"Yes, I want to pay my respects to Mrs. Baggert. But I can't get over your accident and the kidnapping of Ned. Why, bless my——"

But Mr. Damon had no time to complete his pet phrase, for half way up the path to the house Tom and his friend saw an old man coming toward them, ragged and unkempt—a veritable tramp. He held in his outstretched hand a dirty piece of paper.

"Is this Mr. Tom Swift?" asked the ragged man, looking at Mr. Damon.

"No, I am," answered the owner of the name.

"Then I have a strange message for you," went on the tramp in whining tones. "And if you see fit to reward me for bringing it, I'd be glad, for I'm a poor old codger and I'm hungry——"

Tom Swift hastily took the dirty piece of paper and uttered an exclamation of surprise as he read what was scrawled on it.

CHAPTER V

ON A MYSTERIOUS TRAIL

"WHAT's the matter, Tom?" asked Mr. Damon, for he could not fail to note the agitation of the young inventor on reading the strange message brought by so strange a messenger. "Bless my favorite detective story, but you act as though you had news!"

"I hope it proves to be good news and true news," said Tom, looking sharply at the whining old man. "Read that, Mr. Damon!"

Tom thrust the dirty piece of paper into the extended hand of the eccentric man. Slowly, for the writing was not very clear, Mr. Damon read:

"Take this to Tom Swift and receive ten dollars. Help. Am prisoner at Smith place. Brick house—flat roof—three cherry trees—old stone well. Ned Newton."

"Why—why—" faltered Mr. Damon, turning

45

the paper over, "it's from—from Ned Newton, who's missing.   It's from him!"

"It *purports* to be," said Tom in a low voice, looking at the old man who was rubbing with a lean hand a chin very much in need of the good offices of a razor.   "But it may be a hoax."

"Is it Ned's writing?" asked Mr. Damon.

"Let me look at it again," suggested the young inventor.   "I was so surprised by the import of the message that I didn't pay much attention to the handwriting."   He scrutinized it closely and said in a low voice to his odd friend: "It's Ned's scribbling all right.   No one else makes a capital N just like Ned.   Where did you get this?" he asked the old man sharply.

"In a field, boss.   I picked it up and I made out to read it.   I saw your name on it and I made some inquiries and folks directed me here.   It's been a long walk, and I'm tired and hungry and——"

"We'll see that you don't lose anything by what you did if this turns out to be no fake," said Tom, still a bit sternly.   "It will be worth a good deal more than ten dollars to you if this leads to the finding of my helper.   Now tell me straight, where did you get this?"

"In the field, boss, I told you."

"What field?"

"About five miles from here, over Cherry Valley way. I'm on the tramp—there's no use lying to you—I'm a sort of a bum, but it ain't all my fault. I work at helping on a farm when I can, but there's been so much rain lately I couldn't get much to do."

"He's right there—it has rained a lot," said Mr. Damon.

"Sure it has, boss. I've been tramping around and I was cooking a little meal in a field over Cherry Valley way when I picked up this paper. I can read—I went to school once," he said, with a flash of pride, but it was only a brief flash. "I read what it said and I asked my way here."

"How did the paper get in the field?" asked Tom. "Did it blow there?"

"No, boss, it come down on a kite."

"On a *kite?*" cried Mr. Damon. "Bless my phonograph, but he's hoaxing you, Tom! Pay no attention to him. It's all a trick to get money out of you."

But the old man did not appear to be one who would play a joke, and his face was grave as he made the surprising statement about the kite. Also there was about him a pathetic, hungry, hoping look as he glanced at Tom Swift.

"You say this message came down in a field on a *kite?*" asked Tom, and his voice though at first stern, was now kinder, for he felt sorry for the old codger.

"Yes, boss, in a field where I was roasting some ears of corn a farmer said I could have. They was almost roasted when down out of the air swooped this kite. First I thought some boys must 'a' been playing around there and it got away from them. But I didn't see no boys. Then I picked up the kite and this message was on it."

"You mean this message was tied to the tail or to the string of the kite itself?"

"No, it wasn't tied on. It was part of the kite—part of the paper the kite was made of. There wasn't no string to speak of. Looked to me like the kite broke away. This message was writ right on the paper of the kite. It was partly tore off so I finished ripping it loose, and put it in my pocket."

"Where's the remainder of the kite?" asked Tom. He was going to prove this strange tale to the very bottom.

"Here 'tis." The shuffling old tramp drew from a pocket of his ragged coat a tangled mass of broken sticks, brown paper and string.

Tom took the tattered stuff and smoothed it out. Slowly he assembled it into a small kite of the kind that needs no tail to be sent up, a curve of the cross stick and the consequent bellying of the loose paper serving to hold the wind against the kite's surface. From the center of the kite a piece of the paper had been torn. This piece was represented by the fragment containing the message appealing for help. Tom fitted it in and proved that this part of the old tramp's tale was true.

"It looks as if there might be something in it, Tom," said Mr. Damon.

"Yes. But whether this will help us find Ned or not is another question. You say this kite was blown to where you were in the field?" Tom asked the old fellow.

"Yes, boss. It come down right near my fire."

"From which direction?"

The tramp considered for a moment and answered.

"Right from the south."

Tom knew that the prevailing winds at this time of year in the vicinity of Shopton, where he lived, were from the south. So far the tramp had not tripped himself up.

"What do you make of it, Tom?" asked the eccentric man as he began an examination of the remains of the kite.

"I don't know what to think," was the reply. "This is most certainly from Ned, and he seems to be a prisoner on the 'Smith place,' wherever that is."

"Maybe I can help you out there," broke in

the tramp. "I asked some questions before I started off to locate you, and I heard that about a mile from Cherry Valley is an abandoned farm known as the Smith place."

"Good!" cried Tom. "I'm beginning to believe you, my man. If this works out it will be the best day's work you've done for a long time."

"But, Tom!" objected Mr. Damon who, in spite of his eccentricities was hard-headed when it came to business. "Assuming, Tom, that Ned is a prisoner on the Smith place, how could he fly this kite to ask for help? Maybe this man is just making up that part of the story. He may be one of those who helped kidnap Ned and have brought this message from the captors."

"No, boss, honest to goodness I don't know nothin' about no kidnappin'!" cried the tramp, with vehement earnestness. "It was just as I told you—I picked that kite up in the field at Cherry Valley."

"It may have happened as this man says," Tom said to Mr. Damon. "If Ned is a prisoner in some old farm house, he may be confined in an upper room. From there he could loose this kite and, on a windy day, it might be blown several miles."

"But how could he make a kite and fly it

without being seen?" asked Mr. Damon. "And, when it comes to that, how could he make a kite, anyhow, if he's a prisoner?"

"It wasn't much of a trick to make this kite," replied Tom as he examined the remains of it again. "It's made of a section torn from a paper bag, with sticks whittled off a window casing, I should say. Ned could do the whittling with his knife—he always carries one. Probably they brought him food in a paper bag, tied with a string. This looks like grocery store string," he added, pulling out some strands from the tangled mess of sticks and paper.

"I see, Tom."

"Well, having decided to the best of our knowledge that this message really comes from Ned and that he is a prisoner at the Smith place, the next thing to do is to rescue him. Will you come with us and show us just where you picked up this message kite?" he asked the old tramp.

"Sure I will, boss, but I'm——"

"I know! You're tired and hungry!" interrupted the young inventor. "I'll see that you get a rest and some food, and you'll be paid well. We can't start at once—a few preparations are necessary. We've got to organize a searching party and hit the trail after Ned."

"And I'm going with you!" cried Mr. Damon. "No, not a word—don't forbid me!" he begged as he saw Tom hesitate. "I'm going!"

"As you think best," Tom Swift agreed. "But we'll have to do considerable before we can get ready. I think I'll take Koku along," he said.

"Good idea!" chuckled Mr. Damon. "He'll be a match for any four men that may be holding Ned a prisoner. But why did they capture him, Tom? Answer me that!"

"I wish I could," was the musing answer. "I don't know what to think. I'm afraid there's a deeper plot in all this than I had any idea of at first. Starting with the attempt to blow me up, then Ned's disappearance—I'm afraid it means that some one objects, very strongly, to my perfecting—well, what I am perfecting," Tom concluded, not wishing to name his latest invention.

"Well, let's get going!" begged Mr. Damon, with the eagerness and enthusiasm of a boy. "Now don't you run away!" he playfully ordered the old tramp.

"Not much chance of that, boss. I'm too weak hardly to walk, let alone running."

"We'll soon fix you up," declared Tom, "in the way of food, anyhow. And you won't need to walk. We'll go in my electric runabout to the Smith place and get Ned out of the hands of these scoundrels."

In spite of Tom's haste in making preparations, it was not until the next morning that he was able to take the mysterious trail that he hoped would lead to his kidnapped chum. In the first place, the old tramp was really so weak from lack of food and from his long walk that Dr. Layton said it would not be wise to start out with him as a guide until he had had a night's rest and plenty of nourishing food.

Then a slight accident occurred in one of the shops and Tom had to straighten that out. It was not serious, however. So, early the morning following the receipt of the kite message, Tom, with Mr. Damon, Koku and Bill Tagg, as the tramp called himself, started off in the speedy electric runabout for Cherry Valley.

Just as they were about to leave, Jacob Greenbaum came hurrying out of the private laboratory.

"Are you going away, Mr. Swift?" the man asked.

"Yes," Tom answered, though he gave no further particulars. The attempt to rescue Ned was being kept secret. No information was given out concerning the identity of the strange tramp, Bill Tagg, and, aside from a private message conveyed to Mr. and Mrs. Newton that

Ned had been heard from, nothing was said about the strange clue. "Yes, Greenbaum, I am going away for a little trip. Is there anything you wanted to see me about?"

"Yes, Mr. Swift, there is. I've reached a critical point in this magnetic gear shift model and if you could come in my room——"

There was a strange look in the man's eyes— a look Tom Swift did not like. The man seemed unduly eager to get Tom out of the auto and back into the laboratory.

"I haven't time, Greenbaum," the young inventor said. "I'll see you when I get back. That gear shift will keep." With that Tom turned on the current and the runabout speeded down the drive. A look back over his shoulder showed the man still standing there, with that same eager, tense look on his face.

"I think," said Tom to himself, "that my suspicions of you will soon be justified, Greenbaum. But just now I'm on the trail of Ned Newton!"

The motors hummed more shrilly as the runabout gathered speed.

CHAPTER VI

TOO LATE

"THIS is a pretty slick little car, boss," said Tagg when they had passed the confines of Shopton and were heading out into the country. "She sure can go! Beats old Shanks' mare," and he looked down at his legs which had carried him to Tom's home with the mysterious message.

The tramp had been provided with some decent clothes, he had taken a bath and shaved, and was quite a different looking man from the one who first encountered Mr. Damon and Tom.

"Yes," admitted the young inventor as he listened to the hum of the small but powerful motors as they received their impulses from the storage battery Tom had evolved. "At one time this was the speediest car on the road, but I have some now that can beat this."

"And they aren't in it with some of the airships Mr. Swift has," remarked Mr. Damon.

"That's what I want to do before I die, boss,"

murmured the tramp. "I want to ride in an airship."

"Well, if we rescue my friend through your
help, I'll see that you have your wish," promised the head of the Swift plant. "It's easily
done."

"Gee, boss, but I sure would love that!" murmured Bill Tagg.

"Airship—him lots good!" grunted Koku,
who sat stolidly on the rear seat with the tramp,
listening to the talk. Koku was not much given
to conversation, but when it came to fighting
he was as wide awake and as lively as heart
could wish. Tom had brought the giant along
in case there should be a fight, which seemed
likely. Men who go to the length of kidnapping
seldom stop there in their desperate ventures.
"Lots good—airships!" rumbled Koku in his
deep voice.

"You ought to know. You came from your
country of giants in one," chuckled Mr. Damon,
for he well remembered that exciting trip, the
details of which will be found set down in another volume.

Tom knew the road to Cherry Valley, and it
did not take long, in his speedy car, to arrive in
the vicinity. The entrance to the valley led up
a long hill, and the car was half way over this
rather stiff climb when there was a sudden

grinding noise from the machinery and the run-about stopped.

"Something wrong!" cried Mr. Damon.

"Sounds that way," admitted Tom as he made a quick turn and let the car back slowly down against a tree at the side of the road where it was held safely from rolling farther in case the brakes did not hold. In an instant the young inventor was out and peering into the interior of his runabout.

"Dirty work here!" he exclaimed as he pulled out a twisted piece of metal. "See what was in the gears!"

"What?" asked Mr. Damon, who did not know much about machinery, as you can guess when you read how he managed the first motor-cycle he bought. "What is it?"

"A screw driver!" exclaimed Tom. "It was put in here, suspended on a piece of rope in such a manner that the rope would gradually wear through, letting the screw driver drop into the gears. And that's just what happened! One set of gears is chewed to nothing!"

"That's bad!" said Mr. Damon. His scant knowledge of machinery was sufficient for him to understand that something vitally wrong had happened to the car, even if the serious look on Tom's face had not informed him of the same fact. "How did it happen?"

"It didn't happen—it was caused!" was the answer. "Some one, just before we started out, suspended this screw driver in the gear box knowing that after we had run a few miles the rope would wear through and the thing would drop. Dirty work!"

"You seem to be getting a lot of bad breaks lately, Tom," said the odd man. "Who do you suppose did this?"

"I think it's the same man I suspect of other things," was the reply. "I'm going to find out."

"Are we stuck, Tom? Can't we go on and rescue Ned?" Mr. Damon inquired.

"Oh, yes, we can go on, but we can't make much speed. I'll have to run in third. Fourth and fifth gears are all chewed up." It was because of its five selective speeds that the electric runabout was such a wonderful machine.

"Whoever did this made a little mistake," chuckled Tom, for he had a saving sense of humor. "If they'd fixed it so the screw driver dropped into the lower gears we never could have started again once we stopped. As it is, we can go on, but we can't make speed."

It did not take him long to cut out the two higher gearing mechanism attachments, and then the runabout proceeded again. Even at the lowered rate its speed was better than that of many gasoline automobiles. And in due time the head of the slope was reached. Before the searchers lay Cherry Valley which, they hoped, contained the Smith place and the captive Ned Newton.

"Now, Tagg, show us the field where you saw the kite come down," requested Tom when they were driving along a level road.

"It's about a mile farther on," the tramp said, looking about for landmarks. "Yes, just about a mile."

This distance was soon covered, and when the car was stopped Tagg led the way into the field and showed where he had built a fire to roast ears of corn. The blackened ashes and the remains of his feast proved that, so far, he had spoken the truth. Then he showed just where he had picked up the broken kite, and some fragments of the brown bag paper which bore Ned's message were found among the hills of corn.

"It looks as if we were on the right track," said Mr. Damon.

"I hope so," murmured Tom. "Now to locate the Smith place."

"It's south of here, about a mile and a half," said the tramp. "'Tisn't a very good road, though."

"That won't keep us back," declared Tom, and once more they were on the way. The runabout was doing fairly well in spite of the handicap of two stripped gears.

Cherry Valley was rather a sparsely settled part of the country and as Tom and his friends advanced they noticed that it grew more and more deserted. They passed one ramshackle farmhouse and learned, on inquiry, that they were headed right for the old Smith homestead.

"But they don't nobody live there now, mister," said a slattern of a woman who shuffled to the door in response to Tom's knock. "They ain't been nobody livin' in the Smith place nigh onto four years now."

"That's all right—we'll find it I guess," responded the young inventor, and once more he drove his electric car onward.

Near the end of the valley and adjoining a patch of dense woods, they came upon the Smith house. It had once been the home of a prosperous farmer, but he had fallen upon evil days and the place had long been deserted.

"That's it!" cried Mr. Damon, catching sight of the old brick house. "There it is, three cherry trees, old stone well, and everything just as Ned described it."

"Hush, please! Not so loud!" begged Tom, slowing up his car and guiding it behind a clump of trees not far from the house. "If we're go-

ing to make a rescue it might be well to take
these kidnappers by surprise."

"Bless my ear trumpet, I never thought of
that!" whispered the odd man. "Of course!
Certainly! Yes! Quiet does it!"

"Can you use a gun?" asked Tom curtly of
the tramp.

"Well, boss, I'm not a very good shot,
but——"

"I don't believe there'll be any need of shooting," interrupted Tom, "but there's no use taking any chances. Here," and he handed the
tramp an automatic pistol, reserving one for himself and giving Mr. Damon another. "We may
have an easy time and we may have a hard one,"
said Tom. "But, whatever it is, I'm going to
rescue Ned!"

"Doesn't Koku want a gun?" asked the tramp,
noting that the giant carried no weapon.

"Me no shoot. Me scrunch um in my hands
me catch!" muttered the giant, opening and
closing his immense fists. It was answer
enough.

"We'll approach from four sides at once," decided Tom as they began to creep cautiously
toward the old farmhouse. "Separate now.
You to the east, Mr. Damon; you west, Tagg;
you south, Koku; and I'll take the north side.
When I whistle we'll rush the place."

"Correct!" said Mr. Damon in a low voice.

Waiting until he was sure they were in their places, Tom looked toward the old house. It seemed deserted, quiet and lonely. But from behind the sagging shutters of the grimy and broken windows evil eyes might be peering out.

Tom gave a low whistle. On his left he could hear Mr. Damon beginning to run forward and on his right he caught the sound of the advance of Tagg. Then Tom began to run, and beyond the house he caught a glimpse of the giant lurching forward.

Together the four searchers reached the four sides of the old house, but still there was no sign of life. The front door was on Tom's side and, his weapon ready, he ran up the steps. He tried the door. To his surprise, it gave and he pushed it open. At the same time he heard Koku crash through the open door on the south.

"This way!" cried Tom to Mr. Damon and the tramp. "Rush 'em!"

An instant later they were in the house.

"Surrender!" yelled Tom, though he saw no one. "You're surrounded! Surrender!"

Still no reply.

A hurried search of the first floor revealed no one. A look through the second floor was likewise unsuccessful. The attic revealed not a soul and the cellar was tenantless.

"We're too late!" exclaimed Tom Swift. "They've gone! But they have been here!" he declared, pointing into a room with iron bars over the only window. "They've been here and I believe Ned was a prisoner here. Yes, he was!" he cried, picking something up in a corner.

"How do you know Ned was here?" asked Mr. Damon.

"This is his stickpin," Tom replied, showing a scarf ornament of silver and jade. "Ned's been here all right. But they have taken him away. We're too late!"

"What's to be done now?" asked Tagg.

"Follow them!" cried Tom. "We've got to get Ned back. Let's have another look around."

They looked, but found little to aid them in their search.

"They haven't been gone long!" cried Tom, as they came out of the kitchen.

"How do you know?" asked Mr. Damon.

"The stove is still warm," was the answer. "Come on! We've got to trail them and get Ned!"

CHAPTER VII

A WILD CHASE

TOM SWIFT was the first of the four search-ers to rush out of the old brick farmhouse, ready to take up the trail once more in the search. Mr. Damon followed, then came Bill Tagg, and lastly the big, lumbering Koku.

"Me find nobody can smash," the giant com-plained as he clenched his immense fists. "Mas-ter say maybe I fight. No fight?" and he looked at Tom questioningly.

"There may be a fight yet, if we can catch them," said the young inventor, pausing a mo-ment in the front to look back at the house. "They've given us the slip. If it hadn't been for the accident to my electric runabout we'd have been here sooner and we'd have caught them."

"Yes," agreed Mr. Damon. "It looks, Tom, as if the somebody who tried to wreck your ma-chine had an interest in preventing your get-ting here sooner. They, whoever it was, wanted

to delay you so word could be sent here to get
Ned out of the way."

"That's very probable," admitted the young
inventor.

Again he looked up at the window of what had
been his chum's prison room, and Tom tried to
picture how Ned, in his desperation, had secretly constructed the kite of wrapping paper,
whittled sticks and string. Then the young
manager had waited until a stiff wind was blowing and had loosed the silent messenger into the
air.

The electric runabout was in the road a short
distance away from the deserted farmhouse.
Tom wished he had time to repair it so the machine would show some of the former speed, but
this was out of the question. They would have
to go along as best they could.

The vicinity of the farmhouse was lonesome
and no other building was in view save a tumble-
down barn. Tom, therefore, and his companions were rather surprised when, on coming out
of the yard, they saw a ragged boy in the road
walking around the runabout and admiring it.

"Hello!" called Tom genially. "Do you live
near here?"

"Just down the road a piece." The boy dug
his dirty, bare toes into the soft dust of the
road.

"Know anybody who lives in here?" went on the young inventor, seeing a possible chance to get some information.

"Don't nobody live here," the boy replied. "But there's been some men in here the last few days, only they're gone now. They went away a little while ago in an auto, but it was bigger'n what yours is."

"Oh, so some men went away from here a little while ago in a big auto, did they?" asked Tom. "We're on the track!" he whispered to Mr. Damon. Then to the boy again: "What kind of men were they and how many of them were there?"

"They was just men," the boy replied. "Men like you," and he comprised the four in a roving glance. "But they wasn't dressed so good as what you are—you three I mean," and he indicated Tom, Mr. Damon and Koku. He seemed to omit Tagg, and a moment later the reason was obvious. For the boy added: "They was dressed more like what he is," and he pointed directly at the tramp. In spite of the fact that Bill Tagg had been freshened up considerably since he shuffled to Tom with Ned's message, there was still an air of vagrancy about the wanderer. It stuck out all over him. He did not seem to mind being made use of for this not very flattering comparison.

"How many men were there?" asked Tom.

"Three well ones and a sick one," the boy answered.

"A sick man!" exclaimed Mr. Damon. "What do you mean?"

"Well, his head was tied up in rags and the other men carried him out on a cot. He didn't say nothin', the sick man didn't."

"That was Ned!" murmured Mr. Damon. "Bless my doctor's bill, Tom, but do you think they've done for poor Ned?"

"No, I don't think so," was the reply. "I think they gagged Ned so he couldn't call for help, and they probably bound him with rope. Naturally he couldn't walk, and they had to carry him out. So he would appear to be a sick person. Well, we know how many we have to fight—three men," he concluded. "Can you tell me anything more about the men who were here, son?" asked Tom, tossing the boy a quarter which the lad picked up in his toes after it had fallen in the dust near him. "Did you see them often?"

"I sneaked down here pretty near every day after they come to this old house," the boy answered. "They didn't see me, 'cause I hid in the bushes. But they was funny men."

"How do you mean—funny?"

"They used to fly kites out of the window—

anyhow, one of 'em did. But I couldn't see him plain, 'cause there's iron bars over that window —up there," and he pointed to the casement of the room where Tom had found Ned's stick pin.

"So one of the men flew kites out of that window, did he?" encouraged Tom. "What happened to them?"

"Most of 'em fell in the weeds," the boy said. "They wasn't very good kites—just made of old, brown-bag paper. I can make better kites 'n them. They was made of old sticks. I picked some of 'em up, but they wasn't any good. One flew a long way off, though. I couldn't find that."

"I can see just what happened," Tom spoke in a low voice to Mr. Damon. "Poor Ned tried two or three kite messengers before he finally got one into a stiff breeze that carried it to Cherry Valley. But we are losing valuable time. Which way did the three well men take the sick man in their big auto?" Tom asked the barefooted lad.

"Down there," and he pointed to the western road.

"Where does that lead to?"

"Lake Carlopa, 'bout ten miles farther on."

"Lake Carlopa!" cried Tom. "That's where they're heading for. Come on! We may catch them yet!"

Tossing the lad another quarter, Tom led his friends toward his car and they were soon off again on the wild chase. They had a definite object now, for the lad had given them such a description of the other auto as to make it easy for them to inquire about it along the way.

Their inquiries were fruitful to the extent that at several garages and hot-dog stands along the highway the pursuers learned that the machine in question, containing three men and one who appeared to be ill or injured had passed not long before.

"We're catching up to them!" Tom exulted, when they had covered half the distance to Lake Carlopa. This was evident by the information given at different garages. Whereas at first the fleeing car had been half an hour ahead, it was now but ten minutes. "We'll get them!" cried the young inventor.

Though Tom got every inch of speed possible out of his crippled runabout, when Lake Carlopa was reached they found the kidnappers' car abandoned on the shore of the lake.

"Just too late again!" sighed Mr. Damon. "We'll never get Ned!"

"We may!" shouted Tom. "Look!" He pointed across the lake, and about half a mile out was discerned a motorboat containing three men. "There they are—I'm sure of it!" cried

Tom. "Now if we only had another boat to chase them!"

"There's a feller a little farther on who rents motorboats," volunteered Bill Tagg.

"Good!" cried Tom. "We'll chase them in their own way. Where's that motorboat chap?"

The tramp pointed out the dock, and in a short time, leaving his runabout in charge of the boat proprietor, Tom and his friends were in a sturdy gasoline craft giving chase to the other, which was now but a speck amid the blue waters of Lake Carlopa.

"Do you think they have Ned with them?" asked Mr. Damon while Tom hastily adjusted the motor so as to get the maximum speed from the boat.

"I hope so," was the reply. "We'll soon find out, if this old tub can stand the pace."

"Have we a chance?" asked Bill, who was taking quite an interest in this pursuit.

Tom looked at the fleeing boat. Then he calculated the speed of the craft he had hired. A few minutes of observation caused him to make this remark:

"We're gaining on them—slowly. Whether we catch up to them before they get to the other side is a question. We'll do our best to catch 'em, however."

He made a slight adjustment in the carburetor to get a few more revolutions per minute from the flywheel and then the four settled back for the chase.

Tom's statement about their speed proved true. In a short time it was discerned that his craft was overhauling the other. The three men could be plainly seen now, and a muffled object could be made out in the bottom of the boat.

"Bless my cranberry sauce, there's Ned!" cried Mr. Damon.

"I hope so," murmured Tom.

The chase was now becoming exciting. Every moment they were drawing nearer the fleeing boat.

"Hold on there, you fellows!" shouted Tom. "We want to speak to you!"

"Haven't got time!" sneered one of the three rascals. "See you later!"

Suddenly the boat in front swerved off to one side. But Tom was ready for this and shifted his own wheel to intercept the other craft.

"Look out! Rocks!" suddenly cried Mr. Damon.

CHAPTER VIII

TWO CAPTIVES

"WHAT's that? What's the matter?" cried Tom Swift, hearing Mr. Damon's shout. "Are they going to ram us?"

Tom had been bending over the gasoline throttle in an endeavor to coax a little more speed out of their craft. Now he looked up to see that they were very near the fleeing boat.

"No, I said rocks ahead! Look! Bless my life preserver, we're going to hit them!" yelled the eccentric man. "Look out!"

Then, but too late, Tom saw and realized why the other boat had swerved so suddenly. It was to avoid the rocks. And now the *Gull*, which was the name of the boat Tom had hired, was headed directly for the black, sharp rocks that reared their ugly heads out of the blue water of Lake Carlopa.

"Hand me that boat hook and maybe I can fend us off," called out the tramp.

Tom, however, was sure this would be of no

service, so he did not obey the request. He was trying with all his might to pull the wheel around far enough to steer the *Gull* away from the rocks. But the craft was a heavy one, rather clumsy, and did not respond readily.

"See if she'll reverse, Mr. Damon!" panted Tom, who had to use both hands on the wheel. "Throw that lever back!" and he pointed to one with his foot.

"Yes, I know how!" Mr. Damon replied. He grasped the gear lever and began straining on it. Suddenly there was a sharp report.

"Did it break?" cried Tom, looking at the rocks on to which they seemed about to crash.

"No. They're shooting at us!" yelled Bill Tagg. "There they go again!" he added, ducking down into the bottom of the boat.

Tom and Mr. Damon were both occupied with trying to save the *Gull* from going on the rocks and they could not draw their weapons. The tramp, however, aimed his automatic and sent a couple of answering shots toward the boat containing Ned.

"Look out you don't hit our friend," warned Tom, who felt the rudder gradually coming around, so that he had hopes of saving the *Gull* from a direct crash.

"I fired over their heads," explained Bill Tagg. "They're doing the same, I guess—trying to bluff us!" He fired again, high enough to clear those in the fleeing craft, and again came a response. This time the bullet was lower and Tom instinctively ducked, though he knew the missile must have passed him before his ear caught the vicious whine of its passage through the air.

Then, so suddenly that no warning was given, the *Gull* struck on a rock just beneath the surface. It was a glancing blow, and the rock, luckily, was smooth, or the craft might have been shattered. As it was, the *Gull* careened to one side, and so sharply that Tom Swift was thrown overboard, landing in the lake with a great splash.

Instinctively, he took a long breath and held it, closing his mouth that had been opened preparatory to shouting further directions to Mr. Damon about reversing the craft.

Down into the depths sank Tom, while the *Gull,* whose speed was not slackened, slued around from her impact on the rock and shot off on a tangent in a direction directly opposite from that taken by the *Turtle,* the boat containing the three roughly attired men and that silent, wrapped figure in the bottom—a figure that was supposed to be Ned Newton.

"Bless my steamship ticket!" yelled Mr Damon, "where's Tom?"

"Overboard!" yelled the tramp. "And I can't swim!"

"Me get him!" shouted Koku, peeling off his coat preparatory to a dive over the side.

"Stay where you are!" came the stern command from the other boat which had circled around and was now headed for the place where Tom Swift's head appeared in the watery circles caused by his plunge. "We'll drill the first man that goes overboard!"

Two of the rascals stood in the bow with leveled weapons, while the third was steering the boat straight toward Tom.

"They're going to ram him!" gasped the tramp. He did not seem capable of doing anything to help, and Koku, being now without a weapon, was of no service. Mr. Damon had laid aside his pistol to work the reverse lever and, even if he could have recovered it, there was a question as to his ability to use it.

Thus fate favored the rascals, and Mr. Damon and his two companions were forced to see themselves being carried farther and farther away from the *Turtle* as the *Gull*, whose engine was still running, headed away from the rocks. Apparently little damage had been done by striking the obstruction.

From a distance Mr. Damon, the tramp, and the giant watched to see what would happen to

Tom Swift. At first it seemed as though he was going to be run down by the unprincipled men in the *Turtle*. But they had other plans in mind and, reaching the swimming inventor, the two men in the bow reached over, grasped him, and pulled him in. He could not fight back, and, indeed, having gone overboard with all his clothes on, was having a hard struggle to keep afloat. Rescue, even at the hands of the enemy, was welcome.

"They've got him!" gasped Mr. Damon.

"We go take him away!" growled Koku. "Make boat go odder way, Mr. Damon—we get Master Tom."

"I—I'm afraid I don't know how to operate this craft," confessed the eccentric man. "I might run it back on the rocks."

Once Tom was hauled, dripping wet, aboard the *Turtle*, the boat was put about and went speeding off and away from the *Gull* which, to tell the truth, was headed back toward her own dock.

Tom, as he was pulled over the side, had a glimpse of the *Gull* going back where she came from. He remembered that neither Mr. Damon nor Koku could operate the craft without some one along to advise them, and the young inventor had doubts about the tramp's navigating ability in the emergency.

"Well, anyhow, she'll get to shore and they'll be all right," reasoned Tom.

Then he gave thought to his own situation.

"Well, we've sure got him now!" chuckled one of the three men.

"You said it!" echoed another. "We didn't make no mistake this time!"

Tom almost fell on the gagged and bound body of another young man, and it needed but a glance to show him that here was Ned Newton, a prisoner like himself. Ned could not speak and could hardly move, but his eyes flashed a greeting to Tom.

"They've got us both!" said Tom in a low voice to his chum, as he crawled alongside of Ned. "But they won't keep us long. Are you hurt, Ned?"

A shake of the head in negation was the only way Ned could reply.

Then further talk on Tom's part was stopped, for one of the men, standing over the two captives with an automatic in one hand, growled:

"Shut up down there!"

CHAPTER IX

ON THE ISLAND

NOT one to submit tamely to indignities, Tom Swift, instead of complying with the command, struggled to his feet and advanced toward the two rough men standing in the bow of the boat. The third member was at the wheel and, Tom noticed, was heading the boat out toward the wider part of the lake.

"Look here!" said Tom boldly, for his nerve, somewhat shaken by his sudden plunge into the water, was coming back to him. "What's your game, anyhow? What do you mean by keeping Mr. Newton and me on this boat? I demand that you set us ashore at once!"

"Oh, you do, eh?" chuckled one of the men.

"Yes, I do! And if you do it within a reasonable time I may overlook what you've done. But if you don't at once release us I'll cause your arrest, and it will go hard with you!"

"Listen to him!" sneered one of the scoundrels. "You'd think he was chief of police or something like that!"

"Ha! Ha!" chuckled another. "We've got Tom Swift right where we want him this time. No mistake now!"

Tom was beginning to understand some things in connection with the kidnapping—things hitherto a mystery to him. He looked at the men. They were burly, brutal fellows and Tom knew that even if Ned were free to help him, they would not be able to fight these fellows. Perhaps subterfuge and craft were better than a show of force. Tom decided on other tactics.

"Look here!" he said again. "I don't know what your game is, but you're bound to lose out in the end. My friends will soon rescue us and you'll be jailed for this. Kidnapping is a serious offense."

"We took one chance and we got the wrong man," said one of the fellows, thus confirming Tom's new suspicions. "Now we have the right one—that's you—and we're going to hold on to you. We don't worry none about getting jailed."

"We've rich friends that'll soon get us out," said the man at the wheel.

"Shut up, Torpy!" commanded one of the two in the bow. "Close your trap! You talk too much!"

"Aw, you make me tired!" complained the one addressed as Torpy.

"You can't bluff us, Tom Swift!" went on the largest of the three scoundrels. "We got you dead to rights now and you'll tell us what we want to know before we let you go."

"Oh, so you're after information, are you?" asked Tom, hoping to draw the men out.

"Yes, we are."

"What kind?" Tom inquired, trying to wring some of the water out of his coat.

"You'll find out soon enough when we get to the island."

"What island?" the young inventor wanted to know.

"You ask too many questions. You're as bad as Torpy—you talk too much!" complained one of the two in the bow.

Tom glanced down at Ned and, guessing how his friend must be suffering, bound and gagged as he was, decided on a new plan.

"All right," he seemed to agree, "I'll stop asking questions. But as long as you've got me safe, as you seem to have, there's no object in keeping my chum trussed up as he is. Why don't you loosen him and take that rag out of his mouth? Be decent, can't you?"

"We might as well let up on him a bit," said the big man. "As he says, we got him now and the other can't do any harm if he does yell.

We're out of the way now—soon be at the island."

"Sure," assented his companion, and they at once loosened Ned's ropes and removed the gag, for which relief he was very grateful.

"What happened, old man?" asked Tom in a low voice, as he sat down on the bottom of the boat beside his now unbound chum. "We've been all upset over you."

"I've been a bit upset myself," admitted Ned, whose tongue was thick from the effects of the gag. "But, in brief, I was set upon that night after I left your laboratory, a cloth was thrown over my head at a dark corner, not far from your place, and, before I knew what was happening, I was gagged, bound, and bundled into an auto. I was taken some distance and brought to that old farmhouse. The men hustled me out of there a little while ago, and after a wild ride put me in this boat. You know the rest."

"Have you been kept in the old Smith place ever since you were kidnapped up until a little while ago?" asked Tom.

"Yes, they held me a prisoner there. But it didn't take them long to find out I was the wrong man. They mistook me for you, and thought they were kidnapping the great inventor."

"I had begun to suspect that," said Tom. "Well, what happened?"

"Oh, they were pretty much upset when they learned who I was," chuckled Ned. "They asked me a lot of questions about your inventions, and wanted to know how the new talking-picture projector worked. But of course I was as mum as an oyster."

"Did they ask specifically about my new patent?" asked Tom, somewhat excited by this news.

"That's what they did."

"How did they know about it? I supposed that was a dead secret from all but you, dad and me."

"So did I," responded Ned. "But there must be a leak somewhere around your shop. Perhaps a spy."

"I believe there is!" exclaimed Tom.

"I tried to escape, but I couldn't," said Ned. "Even though they found out I was the wrong man, they still held me. I was kept in an upper room with barred windows. Then, when they brought me food in paper bags, I thought of the kite idea. I sent out half a dozen, but I guess they didn't blow far. I wrote messages to you, hoping some one would pick them up and take them to you. But I began to think nothing would come of it until one day a kite that I'd made went high up in the air and I knew it would travel a long way."

"It did," said Tom. "All the way to Cherry Valley where a tramp picked it up and brought it to me. That was yesterday, and I came as soon as I could."

"I thought you would," Ned responded. "But when, a little while ago, they bundled me up again and took me away, I thought it was all up with me. They must have had some warning you were on their trail, they got off in such a hurry."

"I think the same man who tried to blow me up gave the warning," stated Tom.

"Tried to blow you up!" gasped Ned. "What do you mean?"

Tom told of the explosion and fire, relating the sad tale of the wrecking of the talking-picture machine, but in words that would mean nothing to the three men even if they should hear. But they did not appear to be listening.

"Whew!" exclaimed Ned. "You were as badly off as I was!"

"Pretty near," agreed Tom. "We couldn't imagine what had become of you. Your folks were worried, but I sent word to them about your kite message and that relieved their minds."

"Did you start to swim after me?" asked Ned, with a smile, noting Tom's wet clothes.

"Swim? No. Oh, I see what you mean! You couldn't see what happened because you were down on the bottom here. Well, I was chasing these fellows in a motorboat I'd hired, with Mr. Damon, Koku and the tramp that picked up your kite. We hit a rock and I went overboard. Then they hauled me in, for my boat slued off and I guess headed back for her own dock."

"Tough luck!" murmured Ned. "Well, what's the next item on the bill, I wonder?"

They were not left long in doubt. A few minutes later the speed of the boat began to slacken and, looking ahead, Tom and Ned saw that the craft was approaching a large island. It was known to the young men as a rendezvous for criminals and other unsavory characters. Tom had not visited Rattlesnake Island, as it was called, for a number of years, nor had his chum.

"Are you going to land us there?" Tom demanded, as he saw that the boat was heading for a dilapidated dock.

"You said it!" chuckled one of the men who, Ned said, was named Snogg. The other, and larger, was addressed as Janner. Those two, with Torpy, comprised the kidnapping gang.

"If you leave us here, will you be decent enough to send some one to take us off after you get away?" asked Tom.

"Don't worry—we're not going away!" sneered Janner. "We'll be right with you all the while, boys!"

It was plain, then, that Tom and Ned were to be held captive on the island with the three unscrupulous men as guards.

"Now you can walk along quiet if you choose, or, if you want to kick up a fuss, we'll bind, gag and carry you," said Snogg, when the boat was made fast to the dock. "Which'll it be?"

"Since we can't help ourselves," replied Tom bitterly, "we'll go quietly. But we won't submit to any indignities!"

"You won't be any worse treated than you have been," said Janner. "And if you come across and answer my questions you'll get home all the sooner. It's up to you."

To this Tom Swift made no answer and a little later he and Ned were led toward a rough, two-story house, situated near the middle of Rattlesnake Island, and left to themselves, locked in a room.

"Well, this is that!" said Ned as he sank down on a chair near the bed, for there was some furniture in the room. "What do you think they'll do to us, Tom?"

"Hard to say. I don't quite fathom their game, unless it's to make me give up the secret of——"

He did not finish, but Ned knew what was meant.

"I hope they feed us, anyhow," sighed Tom's manager. "They gave me pretty decent food back in the farmhouse, but I haven't had any breakfast, and I need it."

After this there was silence. A few minutes later the door was unlocked and Torpy came in with two trays of fairly good food.

"The boss says you're to eat and then he'll be up and question you," the man reported.

"He won't get much out of me," snapped Tom.

"Nor me!" added Ned.

"You'd better not r'ile the boss," was Torpy's advice as he put the trays down on a chair.

Ned was very hungry, and Tom Swift, in spite of his rage, anxiety, and his recent ducking, was also beginning to feel an appetite. So the young men ate and then, casually, Tom began strolling around the room seeking a possible chance to escape. To his disappointment the apartment was more solid than it looked. The door was heavy and securely locked and the window covered with a heavy wire screen and iron bars. Evidently the room had been used before as a prison.

But Tom Swift did not give up very easily,

and now he had still several cards to play in the
desperate game with the three men. When the
food had been satisfactorily disposed of, the
door opened again and big Janner came swag-
gering in.

"Well, I see you had your appetites with you,
boys," he remarked. "And now we'll get down
to business. It's you I want to talk with, Tom
Swift, and not your manager that we took away
in a hurry by mistake for you. He don't know
the answers to some of the questions I'm going
to ask."

"Maybe I don't, either," observed Tom.

"Oh, yes you do!" was the quick retort.
"And you'll tell me, too, or I'll find a way to
make you!" The man's voice was an ugly snarl
now.

"We'll see," was all Tom said.

Then began a rapid series of questions concerning some of Tom's recent inventions, including his *Air Monarch* in which he had circled the
globe. As this machine had lately been turned
over to the Government for use in the Air Service, there was no secret about it, and Tom had
no hesitation in telling things concerning it. He
thought it might put Janner in a better humor.

From the *Air Monarch*, the man switched to
other machines about which greater secrecy was

desirable, and Tom refused to answer inquiries, though his refusals did not appear to anger Janner much.

"How's your photo telephone doing these days?" the man suddenly inquired.

"That? Why, most people know all there's to be known about that. It's an old invention of mine," said Tom.

"Is it? But I understand you're using something like it now to make pictures appear inside a radio machine!" Janner suddenly shot at Tom.

At once the young inventor saw the drift of the inquiries. There had been some leak in connection with his recent work on the talking-picture machine, and these men, or this man, knew about it. Tom did some quick thinking just then.

"I haven't any machine that will make pictures appear in a radio receiver," Tom said calmly.

This was true enough. The fire and blast had destroyed the best part of the new invention, though Tom had plans for rebuilding and perfecting it.

"Oh, you haven't got such a machine, eh?" sneered Janner. "Well, I know you have. We're not going to let you spoil our business."

"What business is that?" asked Tom.

"Never you mind. We're not going to let you make a machine that will permit folks to sit at home and see and hear a show without paying the admission price. Not in a thousand years!"

In a flash Tom knew now who were at the bottom of the plot against him. Powerful moving picture and theater interests would not want to see such an invention as Tom Swift planned put on the market. It would bring ruin to many of them.

"You've got such a machine, or you'll soon have one, and I know it!" stormed Janner. Tom knew, then, that he had been spied upon. "And I'm going to make you tell all about it and promise to drop it!" fairly shouted Janner.

"You've got a big contract on your hands," stated Tom calmly. "I'll tell you nothing and there isn't a man or a company living that can make me drop anything I undertake until I'm ready to let go of it!"

"Oh, is that so?"

"Yes, that's so!"

"Well, I guess we can find ways and means to make you!" said Janner in a snarling voice as he advanced toward Tom Swift.

CHAPTER X

THE ESCAPE

INSTINCTIVELY Ned Newton, who had pretty well recovered from the harsh treatment accorded him while bound and gagged, started to Tom's side.

The young inventor, seeing that a fight was imminent, also prepared for it. Though he still felt the effects of the shock and injuries attendant upon the attempt to blow him up, he was in a fighting mood and did not shrink from it.

"I'll make you tell what I want to know!" snarled Janner. "You haven't anybody here to help you now, Tom Swift. You'll either give up that secret and give the plans to me or you'll wish you'd never fallen into my hands."

"I wish that now," replied Tom coolly. "Not that I'm afraid of your hands," he added, bracing himself for the struggle he felt sure was coming, "but I don't like your company nor that of your gang. So you have my regrets already, though as for any secrets I may have, or any new inventions, they remain my exclusive property!"

"Oh, they do, do they?" sneered the man. "Well, we'll see——"

He was about to rush upon Tom and Ned, who stood side by side ready to ward off the assault, when there came a call from the hall outside.

"Hey, Janner! Hop to it!"

"What's the matter?" asked the big ruffian. "Don't bother me!"

"The Chief is on the wire!" came the answer, and Tom and Ned recognized Snogg's voice. "He wants to talk to you. Step on it—the Chief's in a hurry!"

"In that case your affair can wait," said the big fellow, with a threatening gesture toward the two young men. "Don't think you're going to get away," he added. "I'll be back!"

He walked to the door, still facing the two, tapped on it without turning about and, when it was opened from the hall, evidently by Snogg, the big plotter stepped outside and quickly locked the door again before Tom and Ned had a chance to rush him, which Janner evidently expected would happen.

"There was a chance we missed!" exclaimed Ned, when he heard the lock click. "We might have bowled them over, Tom, and gotten away."

"Yes, that idea occurred to me. But it was too risky. These fellows may not intend to kill us, but even if they only shot at us to cripple us something might go wrong and we'd get a bullet where it would do a lot of damage. I think we can get the best of them in another way."

"How?"

"We'll have a look around this place and see if we can't escape—perhaps not now, but after dark. It will soon be night. This room looks strong, but from the outside the house didn't look either strongly built or in good repair. We'll have a go at it."

"I'm with you, Tom. But what do you think's going on now? What was that talk about the Chief being on the wire?"

"It bears out what I have been thinking for some time," replied the young inventor. "These fellows who have kidnapped us are not the principals in this matter. They are an organized gang, but they are working at the behest of others. I could tell, from the way Janner asked questions about my inventions, that he had no real, scientific knowledge. He had been told to ask those questions by some one who did know, however. He made several breaks that I passed over. I wanted to see how far he would go."

"What's the game, Tom? They went to a

good deal of preliminary trouble—I mean kid-napping me for you."

"Admittedly on their part, that was a mis-take," said Tom. "It was me they were after all the time, only you happened to leave the lab-oratory first and they pounced on you. Then came the explosion. Whether that was set to go off and destroy my laboratory after I was sup-posed to be out of it or whether they really wanted to do me up, I don't know. But they've got both of us now."

"Any idea who they may be, Tom—I mean these men?"

"They might be the Hussy and Kilborn crowd."

"You mean that bunch of the *Red Arrow* who tried to stop us from circling the globe?"

"That's who I mean. However, it's only a guess. It may turn out to be an entirely differ-ent gang. But now that we have a little time to ourselves, let's look around and see what the chances are for getting away."

It was dusk, but by the last rays of the setting sun which shone through the window, the young men began a tour of the apartment, seeking any possible means of exit. Naturally, they first gave their attention to the window and door. As stated before, the former was screened not only with a wire mesh, but also with strong iron bars. A search through the pockets of Tom and Ned revealed, in the way of tools, only two knives. Tom's knife contained a small screw driver, and at first he thought he might be able to loosen the fastenings of the screen and window bars. But it did not take long to demonstrate that a much more powerful instrument would be needed for this work.

"Anyhow, if we did get the bars off we'd have a big drop to the ground," said Ned. "We're higher up than I thought."

"We could improvise a rope from the bed-clothes," suggested Tom, indicating them. "That would be the easiest part of it. But those bars were put there to stay."

"Maybe we can whittle away the wood enough to loosen the screws," suggested Ned. They tried this, but the space to work in was cramped, the wood was tough, and when Ned broke the largest blade of his knife and cut his hand rather severely in so doing, Tom insisted that they give up this attempt.

"Let's try the door," he said.

It was now dark in the room, but both young men had matches, Tom's being in a waterproof case which had kept dry during his sudden bath, and with these they made as good an examination of the door and its frame as was possible.

The lock defied picking with the poor tools at

their disposal, and when this had been proved Tom said:

"We can cut a hole through the door near the lock, big enough for a hand to get through, and maybe we can turn the lock that way."

"It's worth trying," Ned declared. "We'll work at it in shifts."

Their captors seemed to have made up their minds to leave the prisoners alone, though voices and movements in the rooms below indicated that the three men were still on guard. Perhaps orders had come from the mysterious "Chief" not to attempt violence.

There was more than enough food in the supply which had been brought to provide a late supper and even breakfast for the captives, and there was a large jug of water.

Throughout the hours of the night, Tom Swift and Ned Newton toiled desperately to cut a hole through the door. With only pocket knives to work with, it was tremendously difficult labor.

It was long past midnight when Tom, whose turn it was at the task, uttered an exclamation of dismay.

"What's the matter?" asked Ned, who had thrown himself on the bed to rest. "Break your knife or cut yourself?"

"Neither," Tom replied. "But we'll have to give this up."

"Why?"

"There's an iron plate outside this door. I've cut through the wood and come to the iron. It's all off."

It was a bitter disappointment.

"We'll try something else in the morning," decided Tom after a moment, closing his knife with a snap. "Meanwhile, I'm going to get some rest."

"Yes, we both need it," admitted Ned, with a weary sigh. "But when they come in here in the morning and see what we've done in the way of spoiling their door, they may take us to another room."

"No use crossing a bridge until we come to it," Tom responded. "I'm going to get some sleep."

They ate a little of the food, and then, bracing a chair under the knob of the door to prevent an entrance without causing noise enough to arouse them, the two threw themselves on the bed and slept the sleep of exhaustion.

Faint daylight was struggling through the barred window next morning when Tom awoke and sat up. There was a peculiar noise for which at first he could not account. He looked toward the casement and then recognized the dash of rain against the glass and heard the roar of wind. It was this that caused the racket.

"What's the matter?" asked Ned, turning over.

"Big storm," Tom answered. He jumped out of bed and walked to the window. A moment later he uttered an exclamation.

"What's doing?" asked Ned, stretching lazily.

"Those three fellows are down on the shore doing something to their motorboat," reported Tom. "Looks as if it had been damaged in the storm, which is a fierce one, let me tell you. They seem to be making repairs."

"Maybe they're going away and leave us alone," suggested Ned.

"They may be going away," assented Tom. "But they won't leave us, I'm thinking. They'll take us with them. But something evidently has happened."

In his eagerness to see what was going on at the shore of the lake within view of the barred window, Ned jumped out of bed. In doing so he overbalanced himself and in order not to fall he had to do a hop, skip and a jump across the room. He brought up hard against the opposite wall, fairly jarring the place. As he stopped his somewhat mad and erratic career he uttered a cry.

"Hurt yourself?" asked Tom anxiously.

"No! But look! Man dear, look!"

Ned's voice was excited, and no wonder! It

was evident that in his collision against the wall he had struck a hidden spring which operated the mechanism of a secret sliding door. For there, before the eyes of the two captives, was an opening, large enough for them to pass through, in a stooping position, and leading to the top of a flight of stairs.

"A secret door!" cried Tom. "How'd you discover it?"

"I didn't," Ned answered. "It just happened. I bumped against the wall and must have struck the spring. What's it for, Tom?"

Into the eyes of the young inventor shone a new and hopeful light.

"I don't know what its original use was," he said slowly. "But for us it offers a way of escape. Come on, Ned! We'll light out while those fellows are busy down at the boat. Grab up some food and come on."

Tom began stuffing some bread and meat into his pockets after hastily dressing, which was a short operation, as the young men had not removed all of their clothes the night before. Then Tom took another look through the window.

"They're still tinkering over the motor," he reported. "It's now or never, Ned! This storm came just at the right time. Come on!"

"But we don't know where that secret staircase leads," objected Ned Newton as he followed his chum's example about the food.

"And it doesn't make much difference, either. It leads out of this room. That's all we have to know now. I think it must have been put in to allow the secret removal of smuggled or stolen goods—possibly bootleg liquor. Probably the stairway ends in one of the rooms below. But as those three scoundrels are out of the way we can leave."

"Maybe we'll be trapped at the bottom, Tom. There must be a door there, too."

"Probably there is; but it's likely to be a sliding, secret door, and, consequently, won't be very strong. We can burst it out, maybe. Anyhow it's worth trying. Come on!"

Then, as the storm rose to new heights of fury, the two prisoners slipped into the secret opening and began descending the dark stairs on their way to escape.

CHAPTER XI

RESCUED

Using the utmost caution, though they felt quite certain their movements would be muffled by the noise of the storm that raged about the lonely house, Tom Swift and Ned Newton made their way through the narrow, dark passage. It was so low that they had to stoop and, as the way was strange to them, Tom, who was in the lead, proceeded carefully. He kept his hands outstretched, one in front of him and the other pressed against a side wall. Nor did he let his weight bear on his feet when descending from one step to another until he was sure it was firm and solid.

The house was not large, therefore the secret stairway built in the walls could not be very long. So in a comparatively short time, though to the two young men it seemed long enough, the inventor came to the end of the passage and stopped.

"Well?" whispered Ned, behind his chum,

after waiting impatiently for a short time.

"I don't know whether it's well or ill," Tom answered. "But I've come to a wall or a door and I can find no means of opening it—if it is a door. So we can't go any farther without breaking through."

"Burst it open, then!" advised Ned with force. "We've got to get loose!"

"It's bound to make a noise," Tom went on, trying the second secret door by pushing on it, thus determining that it was not of very solid construction. "But I think the racket of the storm will cover it. Are you ready for a dash?"

"Sure!" replied Ned. "We're going to get good and wet, though."

Even in the secret passage where they were crouched, the noise of the storm came to them, and it seemed to be increasing in fury. The wind moaned, shrieked, and whistled around the island house and the rain came down in rattling sheets that played a tattoo on the sides and roof of the building.

"Here goes!" murmured Tom in a tense voice.

He drew back a little and when a sudden and louder burst of the storm's fury enveloped the house, the young inventor hurled himself, back foremost, against the door.

There was a crackling and splintering of wood and Tom almost fell, so suddenly was he precipitated through the broken door. Recovering himself as best he could, Tom Swift saw that he had come out into a small passageway.

There was another door in front of him—an ordinary one fastened with bolts in plain view, and the passage was lighted by a window near the ceiling. Ned followed his chum through the broken secret door and the two stood for a moment, listening for anything which might indicate that their escape had been discovered.

But no sounds came to them save the noise of the storm, more in evidence now that they were closer to the outer air. Then Tom stepped to the locked door and, pushing back the bolts, swung it open. He had a momentary fear that it might lead into another strong room, but, to his own delighted surprise, as well as that of Ned, it gave out of doors and a moment later the two escaping captives stood in the wind and rain beneath the forest trees, free!

"That was luck!" murmured Ned.

"But we aren't out of the woods yet," replied Tom.

This was true in a double sense. The island in Lake Carlopa was densely wooded, and, so far as the young men knew, uninhabited save by the unscrupulous men who had kidnapped them. The sinister name of the place—Rattlesnake Island—kept away many campers who other-

wise might have made the place popular. Perhaps, years before, there had been many of the
deadly reptiles in the thickets, but it was doubtful if many were there now.

However, Tom and Ned did not give this a
thought. Their main idea was to get as far as
possible away from the house before Janner,
Snogg and Torpy discovered that the prisoners
had escaped.

"Come on!" murmured Tom, plunging off
into the rain-drenched woods, followed by Ned.
"They may be after us at any minute."

But evidently the scoundrels were too much
occupied with repairing their motorboat, for the
two escaping captives had a glimpse of the unsavory trio grouped about it on the beach as
they threaded their way through the forest.

"Whew, but I'm getting wet!" gasped Ned,
as they crossed a little clearing and caught the
full force of the downpour.

"This storm was the best thing that could
happen to us," Tom said.

"How come?"

"Except for the noise it made, the racket I
produced when I broke that door would have
given the alarm. Yes, this storm saved us.
Don't mind a little wetting."

"A little wetting!" good-naturedly chuckled
Ned. "This is about the biggest drenching I

ever saw—except when you went into the lake."

On they plunged, taking little heed of whither they went so long as they put distance between themselves and the three men. Then, when it was evident there was to be no immediate pursuit, they slackened their pace and began to make plans.

"What are we going to do, Tom?" Ned asked, pausing beneath a shelving ledge of rock that afforded partial shelter from the dashing rain and wind. "We're still far from safe."

"We ought to get to the shore—as far away from those fellows as we can—and signal some passing boat. There ought to be plenty of craft passing up and down the lake, though there'll be more after this storm lets up. We've got to get back to the mainland. There's no telling what mischief this gang may be up to at my works. The three scoundrels here are only part of the crowd."

"I guess you're right there, Tom. A boat headed for the mainland would just about suit me now. I'd like to let my folks know I'm all right."

"So should I," agreed Tom. "Dad will be in a fit when Koku and Mr. Damon go back and tell him I fell overboard."

"They must have seen those fellows haul you into their boat," Ned suggested.

"Naturally, they did. But that won't make dad feel any easier. Yes, we want to get back home!"

However, there seemed to be no prospect of that in the immediate future. The storm continued unabated and no boats passed Rattlesnake Island, at least near the shore the two captives dared approach. They might have had better luck on the other side, for there lay the usual channel, but the scoundrels' motorboat was there and the fugitives, therefore, must keep away.

At last, Ned's watch, which had not been taken from him, indicated noon.

"Whew!" exclaimed the young manager when he saw the time. "We ought to eat, Tom, and get into some kind of shelter."

"Yes, that's so," agreed Tom, who was as miserable as was his chum. "And if I'm not mistaken, we passed some sort of a cave back there. Let's head for it."

They came to a small cavern under an overhanging ledge of rock, and into this the two wanderers gratefully crawled. They did not explore to see how far back the cave extended, but when they found some dry wood near the entrance they built a fire and took off some of their wet garments. As these were hung on sticks near the blaze, to dry out, the young men, sitting near the grateful heat, took out their packages of food.

Luckily, they had wrapped the victuals in waxed paper taken from some of the cracker boxes supplied them for their first meal by their captors. So that now the improvised lunch was fairly dry. It was rather limited in its bill of fare, however, and Tom and Ned would gladly have parted with all the spare change in their pockets for a cup of hot coffee. However, such a luxury was beyond their reach, so they made the best of what they had.

The rain kept up all that afternoon, and once the two were warm from their cave fire and their garments fairly dry, they decided against venturing out again into the downpour.

"It may stop by morning," Tom suggested, "and by morning more boats will be out and we'll have a better chance of signaling one."

"What! Stay here all night?"

"Why not?" chuckled Tom. "Do you know a better place?"

"You win!" agreed Ned. "We'll camp out here."

This they did, gathering some dried leaves farther back in the cave, and in these they burrowed, finding the warmth grateful from the chill of the storm.

It was still raining in the morning, but not as

hard as before, when Tom and Ned awakened and made a very light breakfast. Then, when they were able to catch a glimpse of the sun, which came out about an hour after they had finished their limited meal, they again made a trail toward the shore farthest removed from the dock to which the scoundrels had tied up.

They soon came out on a sandy beach and into the full glare of a hot sun after the storm. The cheering beams of Old Sol both warmed and invigorated them.

"Now if we can only see a boat we'll be all right," said Tom.

They did not have long to wait. A motor craft came chugging into view and by dint of shouts and the waving of Ned's shirt, which that young man gladly stripped off as a signal flag, the man in the boat saw the castaways and headed in toward them. The boatman proved to be Gill Marsh, a fisherman for whom Tom had more than once done favors, and Mr. Marsh gladly agreed to take the young men to Shopton.

"Though what you were doin' on Rattlesnake Island is more'n I can figger out," said the mystified Mr. Marsh.

"We're not very good at figuring, ourselves, this morning," said Tom, with a glance at Ned. They saw no reason for telling what had happened until they had had a chance to capture the scoundrels, for to attempt this they were determined.

In a short time they were landed at a dock not far from the Swift shops, and Tom was soon in telephonic communication with Mr. Jackson, who was both surprised and delighted to hear from his missing employer.

"Ned's safe, too!" Tom said. "Get word to his folks as soon as you can."

"That's what I'll do, Mr. Swift!" said the shop superintendent. "But where have you been? We've had the police for miles around looking for you two. What happened?"

"It's a long story. I'll tell you later," Tom said. "But how are things at the shop?"

"Well, we've had some trouble, and that fellow Greenbaum——"

But there, to Tom's disgust, the connection was broken, nor, do what he would to attract the operator, could he restore it again.

"We've got to hurry back, Ned!" exclaimed the young inventor. "Those scoundrels are still at their tricks!"

CHAPTER XII

GREENBAUM THREATENS

More than ever anxious, as much by what Mr. Jackson had left unsaid as by what had come to him over the wire before the interruption, Tom Swift hailed a taxicab and in it rode to his home, stopping, since it was on his way, to let Ned Newton off at the latter's home.

"Don't talk too much—outside your own family circle—of what happened, Ned," was the warning Tom gave his chum as they parted.

"I won't. But you aren't going to let the matter drop here, are you?"

"I should say not! But I want to swoop down on those fellows before they know it."

Tom found his father excited by the sudden news over his son's safety, but it was a joyous reaction after the dismal news brought back by Mr. Damon and Koku, following the episode of the motorboat chase.

"What happened after I left you?" Tom asked Mr. Damon, who had been pretty con-

stantly at the Swift home following the kidnapping of the young inventor and his manager.

"After you *left* us?" repeated the eccentric
man somewhat dazedly. "You mean——?"

"I mean after I fell overboard," said Tom,
with a smile.

"Oh, yes. Well, neither Koku nor I knew
how to manage the *Gull*, and your friend Bill
Tagg wasn't any better off, bless my rudder!"
said Mr. Damon. "So we just let her run, and
she slued around so much and acted so queerly
after you were taken aboard the other boat that
some fellows in a sailboat came to our aid. We
told them what had happened—without going
too much into your private affairs, Tom—and
one of the men got aboard the *Gull* and brought
us back to the dock where we started from.
Then I hurried here to tell your father."

"Then I got in touch with the police," said
Mr. Swift, taking up the story, "for I guessed
that those aboard that other boat were your enemies, Tom. But the police didn't know where
to look. So what with you gone and nothing
heard of Ned, we were in a great stew."

"I can imagine it," Tom said. "Of course
you had no way of really knowing Ned was
aboard the other boat, though I suppose from

what happened and the sight of the bound figure in the bottom of the *Turtle,* you might have guessed Ned was aboard."

"I surmised it," assented Mr. Damon. "But we had no idea where they were taking you."

"No, you couldn't know that," said Tom. "Well, we got away from the scoundrels, and the next thing is to catch them."

Having given his father and Mr. Damon a hasty description of what had happened to him and Ned, Tom Swift set about the work of running down the miscreants.

The police were notified of the return of the young inventor, and a squad of officers was sent to Rattlesnake Island. Tom did not go, for he felt the need of rest. Besides, there were things at home which needed his attention.

"What was it you started to tell me when we were cut off, Mr. Jackson?" Tom asked his superintendent after the police had departed for the island.

"You mean about Greenbaum?"

"Yes. Is he still here?"

"Well, he is, Mr. Swift; and I hope I'm not going against your wishes when I say I wish he wasn't."

"Not at all, Mr. Jackson. I have no desire to keep that man if he isn't doing what is right, though I must admit that he is a good workman."

"I agree with you there. But after what happened you must use your own judgment about keeping him on."

"What happened?"

"Well, he and I quarreled."

"What did Greenbaum do?" Tom asked. He knew he need not ask what his superintendent had done, for Garret Jackson was thoroughly dependable.

"I found him sneaking around your private room, Tom—the room where you have been doing those experiments of late. I don't know what they are and I don't want to know until the right time comes. But I felt pretty sure you didn't want Greenbaum to be prying in there."

"No more I do!"

"That's what I thought. So when I saw him come out of that room the second time, after you had gone to find Ned, I called him to account for it."

"What did he say?"

"That you told him to go in there to experiment."

"That was untrue!" cried Tom.

"So I guessed. So I took the liberty of putting a new lock on the place—a lock that fellow couldn't pick if he wanted to, and he came at me hot and heavy. We had a quarrel, and I'm glad you're here to settle it."

"And I'll settle it mighty quick!" exclaimed Tom. He was in his private office now, in a part of the shop somewhat removed from his secret experimental laboratory. Pushing a button that summoned a messenger, Tom bade the boy send Greenbaum in. And when the man sauntered in, smiling and seeming very confident of himself, the young inventor said:

"Get your time from the cashier and pack your things."

"What for?" demanded Greenbaum, with a quick change of countenance.

"Because you're through here."

"Through, Mr. Swift! Why, you gave me a contract and you can't fire me off-hand this way without telling me why! It isn't fair!"

"It's fair enough, and you know it!" declared Tom. "The only contract you had was that I said I'd keep you as long as your work was satisfactory. Well, it isn't. It's far from satisfactory."

"You mean on that magnetic gear shift? I can show you, Mr. Swift, that——"

"No, it isn't the gear shift. I'm going to drop that. It's your own private work of trying to sneak in and fathom my secrets. That's all.

You are through. Get your time and clear out! Mr. Jackson was right in his surmise."

"Oh, so Jackson has been talking about me, has he?"

"I'm not answering any of your questions," retorted Tom. "The sooner you leave the premises the better. And don't come back!"

For a moment Greenbaum stood looking squarely at Tom Swift whose eyes never faltered under the gaze of the angry man. Then Greenbaum asked with great deliberation:

"Is that your last word, Mr. Swift?"

"Yes."

"Well, all I've got to say is that maybe you'll be sorry for this some day! Maybe you'll be sorry!"

There was a distinct threat in Greenbaum's words.

"What do you mean?" cried Tom in anger starting from his chair. "How dare you threaten me?"

Greenbaum made no answer, but turned and went out of the office. Tom was about to follow, for he did not want the fellow to think he could thus defy him, when the telephone on the desk rang out sharply.

CHAPTER XIII

MR. DAMON DANCES

"Hello! Hello!" the young inventor called into the transmitter. "What is it?"

He did not recognize the voice at first, but the speaker soon identified himself as Joe Corrigan, the officer in charge of the squad of men who had gone to Rattlesnake Island in an endeavor to apprehend the three men.

"But they had flew the coop, Mr. Swift," reported Joe Corrigan. "Not hide nor hair of 'em on the place."

"Did you find the house?"

"Oh, sure! And we saw where you and Mr. Newton broke out. But the men must have skipped right after they found you had got away."

"I suppose so. What about their boat?"

"No trace of that, either. I'm sorry we didn't get 'em!"

"I hardly thought you would—it was just a chance," Tom retorted.

"But we're not going to give up," declared Corrigan. "We'll catch 'em yet!"

Tom had his doubts on this subject, but he did not express them.

"Wish you lots of luck!" he called over the wire.

He was sure, however, that Snogg, Janner and Torpy were but the tools in the hands of more powerful men, men who would keep themselves well hidden, and that though the ruffians might be apprehended in time, little or nothing would be learned from them. They would take the blame and say nothing of the men who had hired them, probably being well paid for any punishment they might suffer.

"Well, so much for that," said Tom when he had ruminated over what Corrigan had reported. "Now about Greenbaum. That's more serious. I can't let him get away with threatening me like that."

However, when Tom hurried out to intercept Greenbaum he found that the fellow had packed his belongings and hurried away.

"That was quick work," reflected Tom. Then, as he thought the matter over, he was pretty sure that Greenbaum had anticipated what was coming to him and had accordingly made his arrangements for a speedy departure. "I only hope he didn't get into the laboratory to do more damage to my talking-picture machine before he lighted out."

He was reassured, however, when he found Koku on guard at the door of the laboratory which still needed a bit of work to restore it to the spick-and-span condition it was in before the explosion.

"Did anybody try to get in here just now, Koku?" asked Tom, thinking the giant might have prevented Greenbaum from a last and dangerous call.

"Nobody come right away," the giant reported. "But yesterday him try come in and Mr. Jackson say I to stay here. So Koku stay."

"That's the idea!" exclaimed Tom approvingly. "Don't let any one in here except my father, Ned Newton or me—not even Mr. Jackson for a while. Those scoundrels might get hold of my superintendent and try to torture something out of him if they thought he knew," Tom said to himself. "It's best to keep the secret among as few as possible until I'm ready to spring it. I want you to guard this place well, Koku," went on Tom. "Especially at night."

"Me guard!" grunted the giant. "Nobody git past without me punch him—but no punch you, Master, nor Mr. Ned."

"No, please don't punch us, or my father,"

begged Tom, with a smile. Well he knew the weight of that mighty fist.

Thinking it not worth while to follow the man, Tom posted a notice to the effect that Greenbaum had been discharged and gave orders that he was not again to be admitted to the works on any pretext.

For the last few years the Swift plant had been surrounded by a high and strong fence, which was further defended against marauders by electrically charged wires. These wires did not carry a high enough current, under ordinary circumstances, to cause death, but the shock they could administer to unauthorized persons seeking to gain admittance was severe enough to deter them.

Having seen to the safety of the plant in general, Tom, after telephoning to Ned the result of the police visit to Rattlesnake Island, began to prepare for the resumption of work on his talking-picture apparatus. It was not long before the destroyed parts had been remade and he was about ready to start experimenting again.

"Well, Ned," said Tom to his helper one day about two weeks after their strenuous experiences, "are you ready to be an actor again?"

"You mean in the song and dance line—trying

to make my voice and image come through solid walls?"

"That's the idea. I have my machine set up again after the explosion, and I think I'm nearer the solution than ever before. I've made a lot of changes. In a way, the fire and blast didn't mean such a total loss, after all. It helped put me on a new track."

"That's good. Well, I'm ready for you as soon as I get this statement off to the bank. What's the idea, Tom, borrowing so much money on notes?"

"Got to have it, Ned," and the young inventor seemed a bit put out by the question.

"Is it for this new invention?"

"Yes."

"Well, why not sell some of your securities? Money is high now, and to borrow it I've got to make statements to the bank that disclose a lot of your private dealings. Of course, they're in safe hands, but——"

"Go ahead and get the money, Ned. We'll need all that and more. I've sunk a lot in this invention, but I'll get it all back again, and more too. No use spoiling the ship for a pennyworth of tar, you know."

"Yes, I know, Tom. And if you're sure you're on the right track——"

"I'm never sure of anything in this world, Ned. But I know one thing, if I don't pull out of this a winner, the banks will be asking a lot more questions than they have."

"As bad as that?" asked Ned, struck by his friend's serious manner.

"As bad—or as good. It depends on how you look at it. But I'll leave the finances to you. I'm going to try out some new ideas now as soon as you can get into the broadcasting room."

Tom called the room where Ned did his acting under the battery of electric lights his "broadcasting studio." In a measure this was what it was, for vocal sounds and instrumental music were broadcast from it in the manner familiar to all who own a radio set.

But what Tom was trying to do, and which he found not at all easy, was to broadcast the sight of Ned and the song, making sight and sound synchronized. He wanted to perfect a radio receiver with an added apparatus by which, on a screen attached to the sounding cabinet, a person could view the person or persons doing the singing, dancing, or whatever form of activity was being presented.

This of course was not to be confounded with some moving and "talking" pictures, which are a combination of films and phonograph records, working simultaneously. By Tom's machine.

when perfected, one would be enabled to see and hear an actual theater play, a complete vaudeville show, or even a complete operatic performance.

When Ned finished his financial work he went to the studio and there he remained until far into the night while Tom, in his laboratory, watched the metallic glass screen and changed and adjusted switches, eliminators, tubes and different forms of electrical currents, endeavoring to capture not only Ned's voice but his image.

"Well, how did it go, Tom?" asked Ned, coming to the laboratory after a bell signal told him work for the night was over.

"Somewhat better, I'm glad to say. I could see you much more plainly. Your voice was very clear. It's only the vision apparatus that needs improving. How did you make out?"

"Oh, I don't mind it. But why did you send some one to look through the windows at me?"

"Look through the windows at you?" exclaimed Tom. "I didn't! You must be dreaming!"

"Indeed, I'm not. Two or three times, while I was singing and dancing, I saw faces peering in at me. I thought you had some men checking up."

"No, indeed!" cried Tom. "Ned, I believe the spies are at work again!"

This seemed very possible when the two compared notes. Though Koku on guard outside the laboratory had reported no suspicious persons around, this much could not be said of the room where Ned performed.

"We'll guard that, too!" decided Tom, and the next time when a "show" was put on, Eradicate was on duty to see that no one approached the windows.

Who the unbidden spectators could have been Tom had no idea, but he guessed they were emissaries from the men seeking to discover his secret.

As the days went on Tom Swift became more and more convinced that he was being closely watched by men who had a vital reason for discovering his secret. That these men were those interested in moving pictures and theatrical shows was certain. Tom realized what it would mean if their form of entertainment could be presented in even the humblest home in connection with the broadcasting of music, once his invention was successful.

It was one night when Ned had been performing a long time and when the results were not as satisfactory as at first that Tom, sinking wearily back in his chair and wondering what was wrong, heard a commotion in the corridor outside his private laboratory.

"No go in! No go in!" Koku's big voice boomed.

"Nonsense! Of course I'm going in!" another voice responded. "Bless my toothbrush, but I want to see Tom."

"Come on in, Mr. Damon!" called out the young inventor, as a new and daring idea came to him. "It's all right, Koku," he went on to the giant. "Let Mr. Damon in. Look here," said Tom, addressing his eccentric friend, "can you sing and dance?"

"Why—bless—well, I don't know, Tom. I used to," and Mr. Damon chuckled. "I once was given to taking part in amateur minstrels. But is this a joke or a serious question?"

"It's serious business. Just as you came along I happened to think that perhaps what I need at the visual sending end is a contrast of color. That might solve the problem, the difference in light rays—red at one end of the spectrum and violet at the other. It's worth trying. But I need two performers. Ned's in there now. He has on a violet suit—regular clown's outfit. Will you put on a red one and help?"

"I'll do anything, Tom, but eat onions. I hate 'em! Never could touch the things. So outside of that I'm at your service. I just stopped in casually on my way home and——"

"You're just in time!" interrupted Tom. "This thing is giving me the dingbats, or it will if I don't solve it soon. Come on, I'll have to pass you in, for Eradicate is on guard."

Ned, who was resting after his singing and dancing, attired in a violet-colored suit, as Tom had said, welcomed Mr. Damon. Tom quickly explained his new plan, and when Koku and Eradicate had made sure no interlopers were around, the new experiments were begun.

"But what's it all about?" asked Mr. Damon as, in his red suit, he joined Ned in the song and dance. It may be said, in passing, that Mr. Damon was much funnier than he suspected. In spite of his anxiety over the outcome, Tom could not help chuckling as he watched the little rehearsal before going back to his laboratory.

"That'll do excellently," he said, as he observed his eccentric friend shuffle about the improvised stage. "Keep it up now, and I'll see how it comes through."

Under the glare of the powerful lights in the broadcasting studio, Mr. Damon and Ned danced and sang while with an anxious heart Tom Swift hurried back to the laboratory to see if the faint image on the metallic glass screen was any brighter.

CHAPTER XIV

KOKU IS DRUGGED

THE young inventor, hastening along the corridor between his broadcasting studio and the laboratory where the new machine was set up, passed the giant Koku who sat on a stool not far from Tom's door. Here the big man had taken his place each night while the testing was going on. With him on guard, Tom felt secure against intrusion by any of the plotters.

"Getting tired, Koku?" asked Tom, pausing on the threshold of his laboratory. "It isn't much fun for you to be sitting there."

"Not much tired, Master," was the reply. "But Koku like do something—smash somebody—fight. No fun sit here nodding do."

"No, it isn't much fun doing nothing, I'll admit," said Tom. "And if it ever comes to a fight, Koku, you shall have a share in it. But it looks now as though the rascals would leave us alone. It won't be much longer now, I think. I'm on the verge of success."

"That good," Koku answered. He did not, perhaps, understand all Tom had said, but he had been associated with the young inventor long enough to know when Tom spoke of success that it meant pleasure for the "Master." For this Koku was glad. "Maybe you make new airship go back Koku's country?" the giant asked.

"No, this isn't an airship I'm working on now," Tom said, knowing it would be of no use to explain to the simple mind of the giant what the invention really was. "But would you like to go back to your own land of giants, Koku?"

"Sometimes Koku think maybe he like to go," was the slow answer. "But Koku like it here, too. Sometimes get hungry for fash," and he named a peculiar fruit that the giants of his land were especially fond of. Tom and Ned, on their voyage which had resulted in the capture of Koku, had seen how passionately eager the big men were for this fruit. They would go to almost any length to get it. And Tom had an idea how Koku must long for some now and then in a land where no fash was to be had. It was a species of melon with a peculiar taste and odor. Neither Tom nor Ned had any liking for fash, but the giants seemed to thrive upon it.

"Some day, Koku," the young inventor half promised as he stepped into his laboratory to start anew the test, this time under different circumstances, "I may take another airship trip to your country and let you have all the fash you want."

"By golly, Master, that be good time for me!" cried the giant with a happy laugh.

As Tom walked over to the apparatus by which he hoped to produce such startling results, the telephone bell on the instrument that connected the laboratory with the broadcasting studio rang hard.

"Hello! What's the matter?" Tom asked, over the wire.

"How long do you want us to keep at this thing?" asked the laughing voice of Ned Newton. "I—oh, dear—whew—I can't stand this much longer, Tom!" and he went off into another fit of merriment.

"Why, what's the matter?" asked the wondering inventor.

"Oh, it's my partner in the red suit!" chuckled Ned. "He's cutting up such funny antics that I can't dance or sing for laughing. How is it coming through?"

"I haven't connected up yet," Tom answered. "I will in a minute. I was talking to Koku. He's hungry for fash."

"For fash!" exclaimed Ned wonderingly.

"Yes. Don't you remember those peculiar

melons that had such a funny smell and taste? The giants were crazy about them."

"Oh, yes," Ned answered. "I'd forgotten all about them. But get on with the show. I happen to have a date with Helen to-night."

"I'll soon release you," promised Tom. "So Mr. Damon is cutting loose, is he?"

"You ought to see him!" chuckled the other performer, and even then Tom caught, over the telephone, snatches of comic songs Mr. Damon was practicing—recollections of his amateur minstrel days.

"All right—get set!" advised the inventor. "I'm going to turn on the power now. Keep toward the middle of the stage, for I haven't got a very wide screen and the focus is narrow. If you get too far to either side I may lose the image and can't tell whether I'm getting you or not."

"Sure!" was the succinct answer of Ned. Then Tom made the adjustments, turned on the power, and waited.

A moment later there came from his loud speaker the tones of Ned and Mr. Damon singing a selection from one of the latest comic operas. The musical accompaniment came from an electrical piano in the studio.

"That's the best and clearest broadcasting I've gotten yet!" said Tom, with satisfaction.

"But that's the easiest part of it. Now will the images of the performers come on the screen clearly? That's the decisive test."

Anxiously, he turned the switch that controlled the projection of moving objects. There was a hissing sound, a slight humming, and then a soft glow illuminated the metallic glass screen in front of Tom Swift. It suffused to a milky whiteness and then, as upon the silver screen in a moving picture theater, but in miniature size, there was projected before Tom's eyes the figures of Ned and Mr. Damon going through the movements of an eccentric dance as they sang.

For a moment Tom wanted to shout in delight, for, perhaps due to the fact that the performers wore contrasting garments of red and violet, the images projected were clearer than any Tom had yet succeeded in getting through by means of his new wireless apparatus.

"I believe I've struck it!" he whispered.

Then he began to laugh, for Mr. Damon certainly was funny. He even seemed to know that Tom, in a distant room, could see him, for the odd man winked one eye and made gestures at Tom as though the young inventor were personally before him.

"Ha! Ha!" chuckled Tom. "I must get dad in to see this. He'll believe in it now." For, up to this time, Mr. Swift had been rather skeptical, though he was fully in sympathy with Tom's aims. "And I'd like to show it to Mary," mused the young inventor, as he sat there enjoying what really was a team vaudeville sketch without either of the artists being in the room with him. Their song, the music, and even the shuffling of their feet came plainly to him through the loud speaker, while the image was shimmering on the metallic glass screen almost as plainly as though Tom had been in the studio. Of course the image was in reduced size. The screen was about three feet square, and life-sized figures cannot be shown on that.

"But in time I can get them full size," Tom decided. "Oh, but this is good! I can see success now, though it still must be a little clearer to make it a positive thing and in natural colors."

Then he bethought him that Ned and Mr. Damon must be tired, for they had been keeping steadily at it for nearly an hour while Tom tried different combinations of lights and currents of various intensities in order to get the best effects.

"Guess I'll 'phone them that they can let up now," decided the young inventor. "They must be tired. And Ned wants to go see Helen. By the same token I'd better give Mary a call, I

guess. I've been rather neglecting her of late—
too busy over this invention."

Then another thought came to Tom—that he
would have the girls and perhaps their parents
come to the studio to take a look at the result
he had accomplished. True, it was not yet perfected; but he knew his friends would keep his
secret until he could complete the patent appli-
cations.

"Yes, I'll give the girls a show," decided Tom.
"They sure will enjoy Mr. Damon's singing and
dancing. Gosh, but he's funny!"

Tom shut off the power. The image faded
from the screen which turned from milky whiteness to the blackness of pitch. Then the voices
of the performers died away as Tom cut off the
radio.

He was about to step to the telephone to advise his friends of his almost complete success
and to tell them to cease their efforts when a
noise out in the corridor attracted his attention.

"Maybe they've decided to quit of their own
accord," mused Tom.

He opened the door of his laboratory and
stepped into the hall. He saw nothing of Ned
or Mr. Damon approaching and at once became aware of a peculiar odor. At first he
could not account for it, thinking, for a moment,

that his father might be at work in the chemical laboratory farther down the corridor. But after a second deep breath Tom knew it was no chemical he smelled.

"It—it's—fash!" he murmured. "The peculiar melon fruit that Koku was wishing for. But how in the world could that smell get here? There isn't any fash within hundreds of miles— yes, even thousands! How Koku could get any——"

He paused. There was a dark object on the floor near where the giant had been sitting on guard. Tom switched on a brilliant overhead light. It illuminated the place where Koku had been sitting, but the giant was no longer in his chair. He was sprawled on the floor, an inert lump of flesh, while, not far from him, was one of those peculiar melons, or fash fruits, of which the giants of that far-off, strange land were so fond.

"Can I be dreaming?" gasped Tom. "How did this happen? Koku must be drugged! How did he get that fash? And what does it all mean?"

As he started forward a noise behind him attracted his attention.

CHAPTER XV

A SINISTER WARNING

LIKE an electrical flash it came into the mind of Tom Swift that there was something wrong here—something terribly and dangerously wrong. The drugged giant—nothing less than a drug could account for the helplessness of Koku—the appearance of that strange fruit, the noise behind—all these were warnings not to be ignored.

So, though his first impulse was to hasten to the aid of the giant, when he heard that noise back of him Tom turned.

He was only just in time. He had a glimpse of a figure gliding toward him out of the shadows, for that part of the corridor was not brightly lighted. And the figure was that of the man lately discharged—Greenbaum!

With uplifted hand, in which was some sort of a weapon Tom could not distinguish, Greenbaum glided toward him. Tom was taken so by surprise and was so off his guard because of

133

what had happened to Koku that he might have fallen a victim to Greenbaum.

But at that moment occurred an interruption and a diversion that saved the situation, and perhaps Tom's life. The door farther down the corridor opened and Mr. Damon and Ned, preceded by Eradicate, who had been serving as guard there, came out. The two performers, receiving no answer to their telephonic signal, had rightly concluded that Tom had finished experimenting for the night.

"At the same time I thought something might be wrong when you didn't answer," Ned explained later.

At any rate, the two performers and Eradicate were now hastening toward the young inventor. In a trice they realized that Tom was about to be attacked. But before the knife in Greenbaum's hand could descend, the man received some missile full in the face with such crashing force that he staggered back. He dropped the knife, and with a cry of pain darted away, being lost to sight in the shadows of the hall.

"Good shot!" cried Ned.

"Bless my rubber boot, Eradicate hit the scoundrel with a shoe!" exclaimed Mr. Damon.

"Dat's whut I done!" chuckled the negro. "I didn't have nothin' else, so I tuck off mah shoe!"

Eradicate had big feet and wore heavy brogans, so the hobnailed sole and heel made as effective a weapon for the purpose as could be desired.

Recovering from the astonishment into which the unexpected attempt on his life had thrown him, Tom Swift turned about and darted into the lower part of the hall in pursuit of Greenbaum. But he was too late. The slight start which the man had, served him in good stead and he made his escape. Though Tom sounded the alarm and got many of his night watchmen on the job, they could not capture the intruder.

Not until it was made certain that he was no longer on the premises did Tom turn his attention to Koku. Eradicate, however, had begun to minister to his fellow guard. Though there was jealousy between the two because each one desired to serve Tom alone, when one was in trouble the other always showed a friendly spirit.

"Somebody done chlo'fo'm him!" was Eradicate's opinion, when Tom and Ned came back from the unsuccessful chase after Greenbaum, to find the giant just recovering consciousness. There was a dazed look on his face, but his eyes opened wider as he saw the fash melon on the floor near where he had fallen from his chair.

"Koku no dream then," he murmured.

"What happened?" asked Tom, when he had sent several men to find out, if possible, how Greenbaum had eluded the guard and the electrically charged fence and so had gained entrance to the private laboratory.

Then the giant, whose immense bulk was proof against any ordinary means of making him unconscious, told what had taken place. He had been sitting in his chair on guard near Tom's door after the little talk he had with the young inventor about his desire to have a fash melon once more. Then, as Koku explained it, a little later, there came rolling along the corridor toward his chair one of the very same fruits for which he had such a longing.

In a transport of joy at the sight and smell of the dainty, not stopping to consider how strange it was that the fruit should have appeared at such an opportune time, Koku stooped to pick it up. But he never got his hands on it, so he said, for a moment later he "went to sleep," as he expressed it.

"You were drugged," declared Tom. "Whoever rolled that fash in to attract your attention and keep you from being suspicious, whoever did that, must have sprayed some chloroform or ether up your nose. You went down and out."

"Maybe so, Master," admitted the giant humbly. "Koku very sorry."

"Greenbaum brought it," declared Tom. "He wanted to get Koku out of the way and then he thought he'd get me. Guess he didn't count on Ned and Mr. Damon being so near."

"He didn't figure on Eradicate's shoe, either," chuckled Mr. Damon. "Bless my trolley fare, but that was a good shot!"

"But look here," persisted Ned. "It's all right enough for you to say that Greenbaum brought that fash here to tempt Koku. So much is evident and plain. What isn't plain is how Greenbaum knew about the fash and where he got it. That's what puzzles me."

"It's a small problem compared to the others we have to solve," said Tom, with a serious look on his face. "What worries me is how Greenbaum passed the guard lines. It also worries me to know that the men who seem bent on preventing me from completing this invention are still on my trail."

"Those are greater problems," agreed Ned. "Very likely we are wrong in thinking these peculiar melons grow only in Koku's country. This may have come from South America or Africa in a shipment of fruit. You know we get pears, or maybe it's peaches I'm thinking of

—anyhow, it's something, from Australia. And if they can ship things that far, it wouldn't be impossible to bring fash from where we got Koku. Only what puzzles me is how anybody knew of these melons."

"We'll consider that later," suggested Tom. "But it occurs to me that the moving picture people have of late been sending men into all sorts of strange countries for travel news. It is entirely within the bounds of reason to suppose that some of them have penetrated to the land where Koku came from and where the fash grows. Some exploring movie men may have brought a few of the melons back with him. You know Koku said they keep an astonishingly long time."

"Yes," agreed Ned. "But that one won't keep long," he added, with a chuckle, for the giant was already opening his big pocket knife preparatory to cutting the melon.

"Not in here, Koku, if you please," said Tom, motioning to the giant to go outside to cut the fruit.

It had a disagreeable odor when whole, but the aroma was tripled when the fash was cut. Koku had speedily recovered from the effects of the drug and was preparing for a feast. If Tom had been a few minutes later in opening his door, the giant might have been dead and the young inventor himself would have been in grave danger.

"Well, let Koku enjoy his fash," Tom said as the big man went out into the night with his treasure, having first, however, offered to share it with his master. The offer was politely turned down. "We've got to investigate what happened."

They could not find out how Greenbaum got in, and Tom began to fear there was still another spy in his working force. He resolved to have a strict inquiry next morning and made a note to charge Mr. Jackson with this.

"But how did the talking picture work, Tom?" asked Ned when they were ready to close the laboratory and disperse for the night.

"Fine! Almost perfect! I'm on the verge of success!"

"That's why those plotters are getting desperate, I guess," suggested the manager. "They're out to do you, Tom. Better clean this thing up and sell it. Then they'll let you alone."

"I'm thinking of that. But I want to make one more demonstration and have Mary, Helen, and some of their folks see it. There are one or two little improvements that occur to me that can be made, and then I'll be ready for a final showing before I get my last patents. After that I'll be ready to market my invention."

"Going to give a sort of dress rehearsal?" asked Ned, with a smile.

"That's it."

A search next morning revealed little more than had been found out the night before. Nor was the strict inquiry the superintendent conducted fruitful of results. No spies were uncovered among Tom's factory forces.

But, omitting no precautions, the young inventor took even greater pains to insure privacy in his personal laboratory. There he worked hard to perfect his invention, taking hardly any sleep for a week, so that he was almost exhausted. His father and Ned helped and so did Mr. Damon. Koku and Eradicate were kept on guard, and the giant, having satisfied his longing for fash, declared that he would not move from his chair again to pick up a dozen of the odorous melons.

And, laboring hard, Tom brought to what he thought would be perfection his newest invention. Mr. Swift was greatly interested in it, though he begged his son to proceed cautiously.

"You evidently have powerful enemies, Tom," said the aged man. "They must think you will ruin part of their business in moving pictures and theatrical performances and that is why they are so anxious to get you out of the way. Be careful!"

"I will," promised the young man. "But they can't stop me now. Success is just across the line."

He had entirely rebuilt the machine after the fire and blast, and it was larger and better than ever. Mary and Helen, with their families, had been taken into Tom's confidence and he had promised them that they should see and hear the performance of Ned and Mr. Damon.

"It's quite thrilling!" said Mary, with a fond look at Tom.

"I hope you'll say so after the demonstration," was his answer. "I may ask you and Helen to perform, also."

"Oh, we'll be glad to," said Helen. "I can't let Ned get away with all the honors."

It was the day on which the final demonstration was to take place. Tom had arranged his apparatus and had invited the two girls and their families to come to the laboratory for the evening.

In the afternoon, about six hours before the time set, Tom was in his workroom putting some finishing touches to the machinery and testing the electrical wires when he heard Eradicate coming along the corridor. Something in the colored man's step and the fact that he was muttering excitedly to himself, roused Tom's curiosity and fears.

"What's the matter, Rad?" he asked, opening the door in response to the faithful black man's knock.

"Man jest give me dis," answered Eradicate, holding out a letter.

"Where did you get it?"

"Out in de yard," was the answer. "I was walkin' round like yo' done tole me watchin' fo' strangers, when de man come up an' handed me dis. He were a stranger—I was goin' to tell him to make his se'f skurse when he done hand me dat."

Eradicate nodded toward the note which Tom held.

"Did he say anything when he gave it to you?" asked Tom.

"He say 'gib dat to Tom Swift. It may be life or death to him,'" quoted Eradicate.

Tom hastily tore open the envelope. As he read the message a cry of rage and astonishment came to his lips.

CHAPTER XVI

A STARTLING DISCOVERY

"WHAT's the matter?" asked Ned Newton. He had been making the broadcasting studio ready for the performance he and Mr. Damon would soon give in there, so Tom could show his assembled party of guests what the new invention would do. "What's wrong, Tom?" he asked again, entering the laboratory just as his chum finished reading the sinister message that Eradicate had handed him.

"Wrong is the word," murmured Tom, again reading the warning. "What do you think of that?" and he handed the paper to his financial manager.

Ned scanned the scrawl—it was only that—words hastily scribbled on a piece of wrapping paper and enclosed in a dirty envelope.

"Whew!" whistled Ned as he read. And this is what his eyes took in:

"Tom Swift: If you exhibit your new talking pictures your whole plant will be blown to atoms. Take warning in time."

"There's no name signed to it," remarked Ned.

"There doesn't need be," responded his chum. "It's easy to guess that this comes from the same crowd who kidnapped you and me—the same men who tried to blow me up. There's no need for a name."

"No, I guess you're right," Ned agreed. "Still, if we could trace these fellows——"

"Oh, I'm going to try!" exclaimed Tom. "I'm not going to sit idly down and let them think they have us scared. Eradicate, show me just where you met this man and tell me what he looked like."

The negro did his best, but he was getting old and his memory was not what it had been. He gave a rather hazy description of the bearer of the sinister warning, but he was able to point out the place where he had come upon the intruder. Intruder was exactly what the messenger was, for, since beginning work on his latest invention, Tom had taken precautions to admit none but his own men to the plant.

"He met me heah," said Eradicate pointing to a clump of bushes near the electrically charged fence. That is, it was electrically charged at night. During the day, when many watchmen were on the alert, Tom did not have the current turned on.

"But I'm going to have it on after this," he decided, when a search of the grounds in the vicinity of the place where Eradicate had received the note revealed no one. "He must have gotten over the fence in some way, didn't he, Rad?"

"I didn't see him shinny ober de fence, no, Massa Tom."

"Well, I think he must have come in that way. Where did he go after he left the note with you?"

"He jes' disappeared, dat's whut he done! He jes' vanished like!"

"He must be a voodoo man," suggested Ned jokingly.

Eradicate's eyes grew round and his jaw dropped.

"No," said Tom glancing warningly at Ned, "what I think happened was that when Rad was looking at the note and trying to adjust himself to the life or death twist the fellow gave to it, the scoundrel jumped back over the fence before Rad saw him."

"He'd have to be a pretty good jumper to get over this fence," Ned commented.

"Yes, but it could be done," said Tom. "But from now on the electric current will be on duty

twenty-four hours a day. I'll put a stop to this
nonsense!"

"What are you going to do?" asked Ned.

"Well, I'm going to take no chances, for one
thing," was the reply. "I don't know whether
this message is genuine or a hoax. But I can't
afford to take any chances. There are too many
men in this plant to risk having even one of the
smaller buildings blown up. If only my own
laboratory were involved I wouldn't think so
much of it. Though of course a lot of damage
could be done to my new invention now that it's
practically finished. However, we'll have the
most thorough investigation possible. I'll shut
down work for the rest of the day and turn the
force into an investigating body."

"I think it's a wise thing to do," agreed Ned.

A little later the big factory whistle sounded
the signal of alarm. Men dropped their tools,
shut down their machines, and gathered at the
appointed places. It was as if, on a ship, the
signal had been given for boat drill. Tom had
organized his men this way to respond to the
alarm in case of emergency.

In a short time several hundred indignant
employees of the Swift Construction Company
were listening to Tom tell of the latest outrage.
He did not need to go into details of his secret
invention which, until it was perfected, he would

not give to the world. It was enough to state that enemies were trying to intimidate the head of the firm in an endeavor to steal some of the valuable secrets.

"There may be a spy and traitor among us," declared Tom. "I doubt that. But there is some way for my enemies to gain entrance to the plant that I can't discover. Now I want you to go over the place. Look for a secret means of entering. Look for hidden wires that may connect with planted mines. In short, go over the plant with a fine toothed comb and let me know what you find."

"That's what we'll do, Mr. Swift!" came the reassuring chorus.

"And if we find any of the scoundrels we'll string 'em up!" yelled one enthusiastic and indignant workman.

"No, don't do anything rash or unlawful!" warned the young inventor. "Make any intruder you catch a prisoner and bring him to me."

The men scattered to make a thorough search, and then Tom went into his private laboratory where his father and Ned had preceded him. He wanted to talk the situation over with them.

"What do you think, Dad?" asked Tom, when he had related to his parent the latest attempt.

"Well," was the careful answer, "to me it looks

like a deep-laid plot against you. They don't want you to put these talking pictures on the market."

"But how is it their business?" asked Ned. "I mean the business of whoever is doing these tricks."

"It concerns them vitally," replied Mr. Swift. "Why, just think what it would mean if a whole theatrical performance could be thrown on the screen in private homes!"

"That's what I'm going to make possible!" declared the young inventor. "Those who buy my machine will not only hear but, on the screen attached to the apparatus, they will see the performers!"

"It may mean ruin to many regular theaters and moving picture houses, Tom," warned Mr. Swift. "Those people have millions of dollars invested in their projects. They evidently mean business," and he tapped the warning letter Eradicate had received.

"Yes, they mean business; but so do I!" cried Tom in a ringing voice. "The question is who means the most business. You don't want me to quit, do you, Dad?"

"No, Tom, I can't say I do. Yet I want you to be careful."

"What's your idea, Ned? Should I knuckle

under to these scoundrels and tell them I'll throw overboard the machine I've been working on so hard for the last year? Shall I admit I'm beaten?"

For a moment Ned Newton did not answer. Then something of Tom's ringing spirit was communicated and, banging his fist on the table with such force that he knocked over a rack of test tubes, the manager cried:

"No, Tom! We'll fight 'em to a finish!"

"I thought you'd say that," was Tom's quiet comment.

"And you can count on me," said Mr. Swift, "though I'm not much good when it comes to a fight."

"Oh, I've got men enough to fight for me physically," said Tom. "What I need is moral backing, and now that I have it I'm going ahead. I've been trying to fight this thing too much in the dark. From now on I'll use not only my own men, but also the regular police force of Shopton. Ned, get the chief on the wire!"

In a short time a squad of police were on guard around Tom's big plant, while, as the day drew to a close and the hour approached for the test demonstration, the regular workmen searched for anything that might give color to the threat to blow the place up.

Just when it seemed that nothing would be found, several of the men, under the leadership of Mr. Jackson, made a startling discovery.

They found where the big outside fence had been tunneled under and, working from there, came upon several mines that were planted near important buildings in a manner that would have done credit to a wartime mining party. From the mines buried wires led outside the fence to a little gully. There, beneath a clump of bushes, the ends of the wires lay. All that remained was to connect them to a detonating battery. Then the mines could all be set off at once and the Swift plant surely would be terribly damaged, if not wholly destroyed.

"They're regular fiends!" gasped Ned, when the extent of the vile plot had been laid bare.

"Yes, they could easily have blown us up but for that warning," Tom admitted. "Yet it may all have been a bluff. They might not have gone to extremes. But I dared not take a chance."

"No," agreed his chum. "Well, what's the next move?"

Tom Swift did not answer immediately.

CHAPTER XVII

USELESS PLEADINGS

Tom Swift was profoundly disturbed by the momentous discoveries that had taken place around the Swift Construction Company's plant. He did not believe it possible, with all his precautions, that so deep and dangerous a plot could have been brought so near to fruition as it had been.

"Well?" asked Ned remindingly.

"Oh!" and Tom appeared to come out of a disagreeable reverie. "Well, there are several things that must be done, Ned. In the first place we must take newer and better precautions to keep these rascals out."

"That's plain enough."

"Then the next thing to do is to go ahead with this thing and push it to a conclusion."

"You mean the talking-picture machine?"

"That's it. After that we'll consider what is next to be done. But you and Mr. Damon had better be getting ready," and Tom smiled for the first time since Eradicate had given him the threatening note that proved to be such a timely warning.

"Ready for what?" Ned wanted to know.

"For the performance you are to give for the benefit of Mary, Helen, and the other visitors. They'll be here soon. It's getting late."

"Do you mean, in the face of what happened, that you're going to put on a program of songs and dances?" asked Ned, in astonishment.

"Why not?" Tom questioned. "Nothing really happened. There was no blowing up of the plant."

"No, but it came mighty close to it. We don't know what hour those fellows set for attaching the detonator to the ends of the wires, and then it would have been a skyrocket trip for us."

"Yes, but it *didn't* happen," insisted Tom, with another smile. " 'A miss is as good as a mile,' you know. We're safe and sound. We are well guarded now and I want to see if my machine will do what I hope it will."

"Very well," assented Ned, with a shake of his head. "On with the dance, let Mr. Damon and myself be unconfined. I'm game if you are, Tom."

"Bless my dominoes, so am I!" added the odd man.

"There really is no danger now," Tom insisted. "I'm not saying but what the scoundrels may try it again. But, for the time being, we are safe. It's just as it is after a hard thunder storm," he went on. "There'll be no danger from the lightning for some time."

"You may be right there," agreed Ned. "Well, come on, Mr. Damon. We'll do our part to make the entertainment a success."

Shortly after this Mary Nestor and her parents arrived in answer to the invitation Tom had sent them, and they were followed soon by Helen Morton, whom Ned greeted with a warm smile.

"But what's going on?" Mary wanted to know of Tom. "We were stopped two or three times on our way through your grounds and made to show the passes you sent us. What's the cause? Is it war?"

"Something like that," admitted Tom. "We're having a little trouble with some men who don't like what I'm doing. But I think the worst is over."

Then, not telling what danger he and Ned had been in, Tom Swift gave his friends a brief description of the new talking-picture machine and prepared them for what they were going to see.

Mary, Helen and their parents took their

seats in the laboratory with Mr. Swift and Tom, while Ned and Mr. Damon went to the broadcasting studio, there to don their red and violet robes. Tom had not yet succeeded in making it possible to render sharp and clear performers attired in garments of other colors or combination of colors, though he hoped, by the use of filter screens, to bring this about later.

Eradicate and another man were instructed to keep strict guard on all approaches to the broadcasting room while the performance was going on. Koku, armed with a big club, and another man with a gun were stationed outside the private laboratory. But Tom did not have Koku and the other guard stationed until Mary and the others were in the room, so the visitors did not see these warlike preparations.

The switches were turned, the wires hummed, the tubes glowed with their strange lights and the black screen became milky white. Then, as over the loud speaker, came the words of the song rendered by Ned and Mr. Damon in the distant room, there also appeared very plain images of the two performers. The transmission was the best Tom had ever succeeded in producing.

"Why, Tom, it's wonderful!" exclaimed Mary.

"Marvelous!" echoed Helen.

"Finest thing I ever saw!" declared Mr. Nestor. "If you're selling stock in this, Tom, put me down for a good subscription."

"Same here!" added Mr. Morton. "It's going to be epoch-making, Tom Swift."

"That's what I'm afraid of—it's too epoch-making," said Mr. Swift, but he did not explain what he meant nor did his visitors ask. They were too much interested in listening to and looking at Ned Newton and Mr. Damon.

Ned's earlier description of the odd man's performance was fully borne out by what happened. At one time Ned had to quit from sheer exhaustion in laughing, but Mr. Damon went on alone, singing, dancing, improvising, telling jokes and funny stories until he had his unseen audience in gales of laughter.

"Well, Tom, how was it?" asked Ned, when the performance was over and they were all together again.

"Very good! But it must be better yet. I don't want to limit the performers to red and violet robes. But I have thought of a simple method of getting around that. Color filters, such as are used in printing photography, will do the trick. I'm not worried about that."

The little laboratory was rather close and stuffy, so the door leading into the hall was opened for air. Mary looked out. She screamed, and turned quickly toward Tom.

"What's the matter?" asked Tom instantly. "Is there—" He thought Greenbaum might be trying some other trick.

"Why is Koku armed with that big club and the other man with a gun?" asked Mary suspiciously. "Is there some danger? Oh, Tom——"

The memory of the kidnapping of the two young men came vividly into her mind.

"There's danger—terrible danger!" exclaimed Helen. "I can tell by the boys' faces," she added, looking from Tom and Ned to Mary. "They are trying to hide it from us; but there's danger, and I know it."

As Ned remarked later, "the beans were spilled then and there," and though he and Tom tried to put the girls and their parents off, there was no denying that something unusual was afoot. The upshot of it was that the whole story of the buried mines came out.

"Tom, you've got to give this thing up!" urged Mary, taking him by the arm. "It's a wonderful invention, undoubtedly, but it isn't worth your life, nor Ned's. You must give it up! Let those men have it to destroy if they want to."

"Never!" cried Tom. "I'm going through with it."

Then followed earnest but useless pleadings

on the part of the young ladies and their parents. Seeing how firm Tom was, Helen and Mary turned their attention to Ned, seeking to get him to prevail upon his chum to cast the invention aside. But Ned was as firm as his friend.

"No, I'm going ahead with it no matter what comes!" was Tom's final decision. "But I'm going to set a trap for these scoundrels and I think I'll catch them. The talking-picture machine must be perfected, in spite of these fellows. But they'll find two can play at the same game. I'm going to set a trap!"

Somewhat reassured by Tom's confident manner, the girls and their parents felt better, though they could not shake off the fear that something would happen. Nor was Tom as easy in his mind as he seemed.

There were refreshments after the demonstration, which had been a success in spite of the excitement preceding it, and then Tom and Ned took the girls home, their parents having gone on ahead.

"Well, Tom," remarked Ned when the two young men were on their way back to the laboratory to make sure it was carefully locked and guarded for the night, "I thought, once, that Mary was going to prevail on you to give it up."

"Not in a hundred years! I'm going through with it. Why, I've got to or face ruin of another sort."

"You mean financially?"

"Yes. You know how much money I've got tied up in this machine. It's all we could beg or borrow or spare from my other ventures. If I scrapped it now, all that cash would be lost. As it is, if I go on and put the machine on the market, I stand a chance to get it back with a profit."

"Yes, I suppose so. The banks have begun to ask questions. I guess it's sink or swim from now on."

"But we're going to *swim!*" declared Tom Swift, with a confident smile. "Give me an even break, and I'll beat those fellows at their own game!"

"I hope you do, Tom. But what sort of trap are you going to set?"

"Tell you in the morning. I want to sleep over it," and with that Tom turned into the house.

CHAPTER XVIII

AN ANONYMOUS ADVERTISEMENT

"WELL, they didn't blow us up," remarked Ned Newton to his chum the following morning after having awakened in the Swift home, having occupied the room next to his friend during the night.

"No, and I suppose we can be thankful for that," agreed Tom. "But they might just as well have had a bomb under my bed for all the rest I got."

"Didn't you sleep well?" Ned wanted to know, though a look at his friend's face was enough to tell the story. Tom's eyes had dark half circles under them and it was plain that he had not rested enough.

"Hardly any," was the answer. "This thing is getting on my nerves, Ned. I've got to do something!" and the voice was a bit irritable.

"Seems to me you've done a lot, Tom."

"In what way?"

"Well, you've invented one of the most wonderful machines in the world—one that will make it possible for a man not only to sit at home in a comfortable chair and listen to the best music that's played, but he can, by a turn of a switch, see theatrical plays. And, not only have you done that, but you've called the turn on the scoundrels who tried to stop you half way."

"I haven't quite called the turn, as you call it, Ned. There is still a lot to do to uncover the acts of those fellows. One of the first things I want to do is to find out how they got in and did their work so secretly. They must have had help from inside," added Tom.

His first step was to set Ned at work on financial matters, to ascertain just how much longer the Swift Construction Company could operate without going to the wall. Its credit was excellent, which was a great deal in its favor. And Tom hoped soon to have his talking pictures in shape to offer some of the machines for sale, or at least to sell stock in a company that might market them to the retail trade. In this way he would be assured soon of a large amount of ready cash. He knew several firms who would be willing to underwrite an issue of bonds, once he could demonstrate that his machine was a success.

Having attended to these money matters,

which were always more or less of a bore to Tom, the young inventor turned his attention to matters of more interest to him. One was to see that the delicate mechanism of his invention had not been disturbed during the night, and the other was to make a more careful examination with a view to finding out how his plant had been mined by the conspirators.

Koku and Eradicate had both slept in the private laboratory, and on Tom's entrance they reported that nothing unusual had occurred during the night. It was the fear that, after all, something untoward might take place that had prompted Ned to spend the night with his chum.

"So far so good!" mused Tom, after he had made sure his invention was in working order. "Now for a look around the grounds."

He soon saw what had been apparent at the casual inspection the night before, namely, that the plotters had tunneled under the fence in order to plant their bombs. Doubtless, they had found out to their sorrow that the wires on top of the barrier carried a disabling current of electricity.

And it was in that way that the gang had gained entrance to the grounds. They had worked in secret, by night it was likely, and had thus been able to plant several dangerous bombs and run wires attached to them outside the fence and into the little gully mentioned before. All that was needed was the exploding spark and the Swift plant would have been a mass of ruins.

The bombs had been carefully taken up and soaked in water. They were then—and this work was only now finished—dissected in an effort to learn some clue as to the constructors. But the work had been cunningly done. Tom suspected that the gang had hired some band of anarchists to make the bombs for them, probably keeping the makers in ignorance of what the deadly machines were to be used for.

Once the bombs were removed, the connecting wires pulled up and all traces of the work removed, Tom had some of his men arrange matters so that a recurrence of the danger was impossible. At intervals along the fence metal rods were driven into the earth and so arranged, by means of electric wires, that any disturbance of the earth near them would be registered on dials in the central watch tower.

"That will keep them out, or at least give warning of their attempts," said Tom.

In truth, as the fence was still guarded on top by the powerful current and now was protected from beneath, there was little likelihood that any plotters could get in. Double guards were posted night and day at all entrance gates and not until then did Tom Swift feel secure.

He then set to work with redoubled energy to put the finishing touches to his newest patent and felt sure he had solved the one remaining problem—that of making visible all colors on his screen. This he accomplished by filters of glass, something after the manner in which colored moving pictures are taken, but using a process of his own that he had only recently discovered.

Though Tom was kept busy putting the finishing touches to his machine, he was not freed from trouble. Every now and then he would get a report from some of his many shops that the place had been entered and things turned upside down, evidently in a search for some of the young inventor's secrets.

"Why don't they lay off and let me alone?" exclaimed Tom angrily one morning after some particularly annoying damage had been done in his airship shop the night before. "What's their game, anyhow?"

"To make you give up, I guess," answered Ned. "They can't get at your talking-picture machine, you've got that too well guarded. But to guard the rest of the plant you'd have to keep a full force here day and night, and that's out of the question with our bank balance as low as it is."

"I realize that, Ned. Yet I've got to do something desperate.   It may take some money, too."

"Oh, we aren't down to our last dollar, when it comes to that," Ned replied.   "But it would be ruinous to be paying a night force as well as a day force, particularly when the former would only be used as guards."

"I'm not going to do that," declared Tom. "It's time, I think, to put into operation my other scheme—the one I had in mind the night we discovered the bombs."

"What plan is that, Tom?"

"It's an anonymous advertisement in the papers, making certain offers and proposing certain terms to my enemies.   Here, I'll show you what I mean."

Tom thought for a few moments with pencil poised over a pad.   Then he wrote rapidly and handed the sheet of paper to Ned.   This is what his chum read:

RAPID young man, who is being held back in his work by threats and annoying, sneaking night attacks, will pay any reasonable sum just to be let alone so that he may proceed with his inventions.   He wants to be swift in completing his work and it can easily be pictured how this talk about making trouble annoys him.   A large sum will be paid for freedom from future annoyance. Answer in confidence, QUICK, Box 123 Evening Graphic Office."

"Do you intend to insert this advertisement in the *Graphic?*" asked Ned, naming the Shopton evening paper.

"That's what I do. Don't you think they will understand it even without my name being to it?"

"I should think the scoundrels might," chuckled Ned. "You have as good as told them by the use of the words rapid, swift and quick, to say nothing of mentioning your talking-picture machine. Do you think that is wise?"

"Oh, they know I'm working on it," said Tom. "It's no use to pretend they don't. The secret is out, but I don't care. I've got the patent rights sewed up now. But I must be let alone in order to finish the last details. Take that ad in, Ned."

"I will. I hope it brings results."

"I think it will," said Tom, with a significant smile. "It's bait for a trap, and there will be some surprises when it springs shut!"

CHAPTER XIX

THE MEETING

Disappointment would have been in store for Tom Swift and his close associates if they had expected any immediate results from the insertion of the anonymous advertisement. Ned Newton went to the designated box in the newspaper office several times following the printing of the cunningly worded request for an interview with the unknown scoundrels, but there were no letters addressed to Mr. Quick.

"I'm afraid it isn't going to work, Tom," remarked Ned, after the fourth day.

"Give 'em time," was the calm reply of the young inventor. "Rome wasn't built in a day and you can't catch these rascals in the first trap you set."

"Then you still intend to catch them?"

"I sure do."

"Aren't you disappointed that they haven't taken the bait?"

"Not yet. In fact, I'm better pleased than if they had put in a reply at once. It shows that there are big and important men back of this movement. If they had been petty grafters or fellows who were just working to get a certain sum out of me—a comparatively small sum— they would have answered right off. As it is, the delay shows they are taking their time and considering the thing from all angles. But I think they'll bite sooner or later and grant me the interview I desire."

"Is that what you want—just an interview?"

"Well, that's part of it," was Tom's answer, given with a peculiar smile. "Once I'm face to face with this gang I'll know what to do. I've pretty well settled it in my own mind that there are big interests fighting me, and, like large bodies, they move slowly. It will be all the better for the success of my plans if they don't bite too quickly."

"Then you're not quite ready for them?"

"Not quite, but I shall be in a day or so. Meanwhile, let the ad run. They've seen it and are a bit puzzled over what course to take, I'm sure."

"Well, I'll leave it to you," Ned remarked. "I've got my own troubles, Tom."

"You mean about finances?"

"Yes. We're sailing pretty close to the wind. You've sunk much money in these talking pictures."

"I realized that when you showed me the figures. But, as I said, it's sink or swim now, and I think we'll swim after I get through with these fellows who are hounding me."

It was three days after this that Ned, coming away from a bank the president of which had suggested that some of the Swift loan had better be reduced soon, stopped in at the *Graphic* office. He presented the slip calling for any replies that might have been received for Mr. Quick of Box 123, and, somewhat to his surprise, he was handed an envelope. The paper was of good quality, though perfectly plain, and the address was neatly printed.

"They're taking no chances of handwriting being traced," remarked Ned, as he hurried back to the laboratory with the missive.

"This may mean business, Tom," he said to his chum, "or it may be a suggestion from some other paper that you would do well to put the ad in their columns. That's a newspaper trick, you know."

"I know it is," assented the young inventor. "However, this may mean business." He tore the envelope open and he had no sooner scanned the few lines on a single sheet of paper within than he cried: "Hurray!"

"Is it from your enemies?" asked Ned.

"I think it is. Read it!"

Ned let his eyes rove over this:

"If Mr. Quick will present himself at a certain house on Rattlesnake Island he will learn something to his advantage. Mr. Quick must present himself absolutely alone. If there is any attempt at trickery all negotiations will be called off and vigorous retaliatory measures at once undertaken. Come this midnight."

"Are you going, Tom?" asked Ned.

"I certainly am!"

"Alone—and to Rattlesnake Island where we were held prisoners?" cried Ned.

"Why not? They won't try any trick like that again. They'll know I wouldn't walk into a trap like that without leaving word where I am bound for and my non-appearance in due time would mean a search. They aren't such fools as that. I'll go and see what they have to say. I'll be there when the clock strikes twelve."

"They aren't giving you much time for preparation. It's after two o'clock now."

"It's all the time I need. I've been anticipating this and I'm ready. Now, Ned, I'll let you into some of my secrets that I've been holding out on you."

Thereupon Tom told Ned something which

made that young man open his eyes. But even at the end, when the plans were all detailed, the business manager was a bit doubtful.

"It's risky, Tom," he said. "I'm afraid to have you go there alone to meet these fellows."

"There's no danger, I tell you. I'm not afraid. My plans have been too carefully made to permit of failure."

But Ned's face was serious, and when Mr. Swift heard of what his son proposed to do he added his appeals to the young inventor, asking him to try some other and less risky method.

"This is the only way," declared Tom. "I'm going to that midnight meeting."

When the time came, Tom Swift set off in one of his motorboats alone, heading across Lake Carlopa in the darkness, guiding his craft toward the sinister black shape of Rattlesnake Island.

CHAPTER XX

MASKED MEN

TOM SWIFT sat at the wheel of his craft, his hands on the spokes and his eyes gazing ahead through the darkness. He had set a straight course for Rattlesnake Island and wondered what would happen after he arrived. In spite of his bold words to Ned Newton, the young inventor was a little apprehensive, as well he might be.

He scanned the water on either side of him for a possible sight of other craft that might be heading in the same direction. But though in the distance he saw and heard other motorboats, none seemed to be laying a course for Rattlesnake Island.

"I wonder if they'll be there—and on time," mused Tom. He did not whisper, even to the unoccupied darkness about him, any designation of those he had in mind. He merely said: "I wonder if they'll be there."

It was not a long run, in Tom's speedy craft,

to the sinister, dark island where he and Ned had lately been prisoners, and almost before he had finished going over in his mind the various occurrences that had taken place since he had begun working on his talking-picture machine, the young inventor found himself approaching the place.

"Wonder if I'm to land at the dock where Snogg and Janner tied up the *Turtle*.   Or am I to circle the island until I get a sign?" mused Tom.   "From the fact that they have named as a rendezvous the old house, I should think it would be at the same dock where Ned and I saw those rascals working on their boat the time we gave them the slip.   Think I'll try there first, anyhow."

Tom was a good navigator, and it did not take him long to get his bearings and head for the dock in question.   As he approached it, he saw a dim light on it and this convinced him that he was to tie up there.   Slowing his boat to half speed, for he was not sure about the state of water, and thinking there might be rocks, the young man stood up and strained his eyes to pierce the gloom.   The single lantern on the end of the dock gave illumination enough to make certain that the way was clear, as far as obstructions in the water were concerned.

"Well, here I go—for better or for worse," said

Tom grimly to himself as he shut off power and allowed his craft to glide up to the stringpiece. The dock was rather a ruin, but he found a ring in a beam and made his rope fast there.

Then, before getting out of the boat, Tom looked sharply about as well as he could by such illumination as a smoking lantern gave. There was no sight nor sound of any other visitor to Rattlesnake Island. Tom seemed to be the only one there. Yet he knew there were others.

"I suppose I'm to go right up and knock at the front door," and Tom chuckled a little. "They don't seem to have appointed a reception committee with a brass band. Guess those fellows don't do business that way. Well, might as well get started."

Before getting out of his boat, however, he made sure that the mooring rope was tied in such a way that, if need be, he could make a running jump into the craft, pull the knot out with one tug of the free end and so be loosed from the dock. Also he made certain that his motor would start at once. It was a powerful and speedy craft in which Tom had come to the island—one that would start with a throw of a switch, not needing any laborious cranking.

"I might want to get away in a hurry," he had reasoned.

Thus having taken all precautions to serve

him in case of emergency, Tom clambered up on the dock and started for the shore end.

As he left the circle of friendly rays from the lantern, he could not prevent a slight feeling of uneasiness creeping over him. After all, it was a risky thing that he was doing—trusting himself alone to unknown men who had every motive for wishing him out of the way or, if not exactly out of the way, at least prevented from pursuing his activities in certain directions.

"But I think I'm going to beat them at their own game," mused Tom, as he walked along.

His feet made ghostly echoes on the rattling planks of the old dock, and, now and then, he paused to ascertain if any one else in the neighborhood were stirring. However, he appeared to be the only one.

"Let's see," mused the young inventor as he was about to step off the dock to the shore. "As I remember it, the dock was to the east of the house when Ned and I looked out of the window and saw the three men. So I must turn right now."

Accordingly he swung in that direction as he started up a path that was partly overgrown with weeds. It was quite dark, once he had left the glow of the dock lantern, and Tom was glad he had brought a pocket flashlight with him.

Switching this on, he let the bright rays fall

in front of him to guide his steps so he would not get off the path. For he had in mind the sinister name of the island to which he was paying a midnight visit.

"They say the rattlesnakes are all gone," mused Tom, as he kept as nearly as he could to the middle of the path, "but I'm taking no chances of stepping on one. I don't want to tread on a tail and be bitten. Even if their bite isn't always deadly, it's bad enough."

In spite of himself, Tom could not prevent a creepy feeling coming over him at times as he walked along on the path. He almost wished he had not selected this means of tricking the plotters. But it was too late to turn back now. He had made his choice.

Suddenly, when he judged that he was half way to the old house, Tom heard a noise in the bushes just ahead of him and off to the left. For a moment he had a fear that it might be the rustle caused by the passage of a rattlesnake through the underbrush. He flashed his light in that direction, but instead of the beams picking up the gliding form of a serpent they illuminated the feet and legs of a man.

Before Tom could cry out or step back, he heard another noise on his right, and there, too, his flashlight revealed the feet and legs of another man.

Suddenly the four feet and four legs made a rush and Tom felt himself caught by the arm on either side. His flashlight was knocked from his hand, but, falling to the ground, still glowed and its rays showed Tom that he had been caught by two Negroes.

"Let me go!" he cried, fiercely struggling to free himself. But the black men held him fast.

Then one spoke, in rather soothing accents, saying:

"It's all right, sir. We don't aim to be rough with you, but we got our orders. I'm sorry I knocked your light down. I'll pick it up for you," and, stooping, he retrieved the flashlight which he gave to Tom.

"Better put it in your pocket, sir," suggested the other Negro. "You won't need it where you're going. We know the path in the dark. And don't be worried. We aren't going to hurt you."

"I'm not worried," declared Tom boldly. "But this is an outrage! I came here of my own free will for a conference and——"

"That's all right, sir," went on the first black man, still soothingly. "You're going to be taken to the conference. That's what we came down for—to meet you and show you the way."

Tom was at once struck by the fact that the

language of these Negroes was above the average. They did not talk like poor, old Eradicate. Rather their talk was that of the man who has seen service in wealthy families. As this was in line with Tom's theories regarding the identity of the men persecuting him, he ceased to struggle and said:

"Very well. Lead me to the men with whom I have an appointment."

"That's just what we'll do, sir," said the man who had picked up the flashlight. "It's just a bit farther on."

The Negroes seemed able to find their way in the dark, which, Tom reflected, was more than he could have done. In a short time they led him, gently enough, into a little clearing and there, showing dimly in the light of the stars, was the house where Tom and Ned had been prisoners.

If Tom had any compunctions about entering the house again he had no time to exercise them. Nor, be it known, had he the inclination. He was there for a purpose and intended to carry it out.

"Right this way, sir," said one of the Negroes, letting go of Tom's right arm and preceding him to the front door. "They're expecting you."

He knocked—whether in a signal code or not Tom was unable to determine—and the door was opened, letting out a flood of light. The place seemed to have been prepared for the reception of the young inventor.

"Go straight ahead," said the Negro who had opened the door, as he stepped back to allow Tom to enter.

Tom walked into a hall, furnished only with a chair. One of the three Negroes—which he could not determine—glided ahead of him, tapped on a door at the end of the corridor, and opened it in response to a voice that said:

"Enter!"

Tom Swift saw before him a brilliantly lighted room. Gathered around a table in the middle were half a dozen men. Each one wore a black mask and through the eye-holes in them Tom felt himself being sharply scrutinized.

"You may go, Richard," said one of the men in cultured tones to the Negro who had opened the door.

Then the masked faces silently regarded the young inventor.

CHAPTER XXI

A TEMPTING OFFER

"Sit down, please!"

The masked man at the head of the table—
who seemed to be the leader—thus spoke to
Tom and motioned to a chair, the only one in
the room that was not occupied. Tom looked
at it a bit suspiciously at first. He knew something of trick chairs—seats that, once occupied,
gripped the sitter in arms of steel. Also this
chair might be over some trapdoor which opened
into a pit or into a tunnel that led to the lake.

But Tom reflected that if the men had con-
templated treachery they could have exercised
their will upon him when he first landed on the
island. They need not have waited until now.

The chair seemed an ordinary one, and as the
leader motioned toward it another of the masked
men pulled it slightly forward. Clearly it had
no mechanism connected with it.

"Well, I'm here," said Tom, as he settled back
in the chair, noting that it felt all right.

"So we see, and we are glad of this chance to do business with you," remarked one, who, for want of a better designation at present, shall be denominated Mr. X. "It did not occur to us," he went on in cultured tones, "that you would care for this method of arriving at a settlement. But, since you have, it appears to be a very good one. We are ready to do business with you."

Tom was at once impressed by something that was very evident. These were substantial business men—men of some culture and presumably position in the world—though they did stoop to desperate means to gain their ends. They were of an entirely different class from Snogg and Janner who had kidnapped Tom and Ned. Nor were they like Greenbaum, though from two or three little signs Tom had an idea that some of these men were very wealthy.

"Yes, I am here," went on Tom, holding himself well in hand and gazing from one masked face to the other. "And I am glad to hear that you are ready to talk business. But there is one objection."

"What is it, Mr. Swift?" asked Mr. X courteously. "If you object to the method of meeting us, remember it was your own suggestion."

"I am not complaining of the place of meeting nor the manner in which I was received," stated Tom. "But I'm not used to doing business in the dark."

"In the dark?" wonderingly exclaimed a heavy-set man on the left of Mr. X. "Why, it's light here. Should we spend a lot more money in having more electricity? No!"

"I was not referring to the actual lighting of the place," returned Tom, with a little smile. "It's bright enough in one way. But when I said I was not in the habit of doing business in the dark, I referred to your masks. I like to see to whom I am talking."

"Oh, so he means that!" exclaimed the heavy man.

"I am sorry, Mr. Swift," put in Mr. X, who seemed affable enough. "But you will realize that at present we must, for obvious reasons, remain unknown to you. Perhaps you would not recognize us if we laid aside our masks, but that we cannot do. There are too many interests, aside from our own, involved in this to allow it. So if you feel that you cannot talk freely under the present circumstances you are at liberty to depart as you came and matters will be the same as before."

"Do you mean," asked Tom sharply, "that I shall be subjected to the same spying observations and attempts made to destroy my plant and my talking-picture machine?"

"I have not said so," was the calm answer. "You are at liberty to put any construction you like on my decision."

"There can be but one decision!" snapped Tom.

Mr. X nodded his head in accent.

"You must take us or leave us just as you find us—masked," he said slowly. "But I repeat my offer that you may withdraw at any time and you will not be harmed in the least."

"No! No!" exclaimed the heavy man, with a gesture of dissent. "We want to settle this business now. It is a big business—it must be settled! I cannot sleep nights thinking what I may lose. It is terrible!"

"You will please let me conduct these negotiations," said Mr. X coldly, turning to the interrupter. "Mr. Swift must decide for himself. He asked for this interview and he must accept our conditions of granting it. Our masks remain!"

"Very well," replied Tom, with a shrug of his shoulders. "It is a small matter, perhaps. We will talk business, as you suggest. You read my advertisement?" he questioned.

"Doubtless, or we should not be here, nor you, either," replied Mr. X, lightly.

"And you said you would pay a good sum to be let alone!" broke in the stout man, who might be called Mr. B, for he resembled that letter in build.

"Yes, I said that," answered Tom. "And I am willing to keep my word. But I may as well say, here and now, that I am not prepared to pay cash. I have used so much money in perfecting my machine for showing in private homes talking pictures of theatrical plays and the broadcasting of opera and vaudeville that——"

"Oh, is it perfect? Will it work?" anxiously gasped Mr. B.

"It works!" answered Tom. "All I need do now is to put it on the market and——"

"That is just what we do not intend to let you do!" broke in Mr. X. "You will not be allowed to do that."

"Not allowed?" came from Tom quietly. "Those are big words."

"And we are big men in more senses than one," said Mr. X, still softly. "There is no use beating about the bush. We know who you are, it is only fair you should know who we are, Mr. Swift."

"Then you will unmask, after all?" inquired Tom.

"No, but we will tell you what interests we represent—if you have not already guessed it."

"I think I can guess," stated Tom. "You are a big syndicate of moving picture operators."

"The guess does credit to your intelligence, Tom Swift," said Mr. X. "We represent many large moving picture and theatrical interests of the United States, and we are frank to say that we see ruin ahead of us if your invention goes on the market uncontrolled, at least in part, by our interests. I admit that your invention may revolutionize our industry. If a man can sit in his own home and listen to a radio program, and, at the same time, see the performers, he certainly won't put on a starched shirt and a stiff collar and pay from two to seven dollars for a seat in the theater."

"And he won't even come to a fifty cent movie!" lamented Mr. B.

"True enough," agreed Mr. X.

"You seem to know something of my affairs," said Tom, with a rueful smile. "You have not missed much."

"We know more than you think we do," boasted Mr. X. "At the same time we realize that you are far from beaten, so we wish to suggest a compromise."

"We are going to make you a handsome offer!" broke in Mr. B, much to the evident annoyance of his colleague. "You will be tempted by it, I am sure. In short——"

"I thought I was to do the talking," interrupted Mr. X.

"That's right. Let him do it," put in two others of the masked men. Each looked like a hard-headed American business man.

"I'll listen to any offer you wish to make," Tom stated. "I came here prepared to make an offer myself. But I will first listen to yours."

He could not help admitting that the men knew more than he had suspected. In spite of the fact that he had tried to keep his invention a secret, the general principle of it had become known to these theatrical and moving picture men. Doubtless they had paid their spies and plotters well.

"To get down to business," resumed Mr. X, "we are prepared to offer you a million dollars, Tom Swift. A million dollars!" he repeated unctuously.

"Think of that, my friend!" broke in Mr. B, who could not keep still. "A whole million!" His voice capitalized the word. "All your own to do as you like with! A million dollars! Think of it!"

CHAPTER XXII

FLASHING LIGHTS

GRAVE though the situation was, Tom Swift could not help smiling a little at the evident sincerity and anxiety of Mr. B. Nor were the others less vitally interested. They leaned forward over the table, staring at Tom's face, which was in the full glare of a powerful light. They wanted to see if Tom would give under the strain.

But the young inventor held himself well in hand. Though he was not quite prepared for the offer, it did not catch him napping. He still had some cards to play.

"Well," asked Mr. X, slowly, when there had been a few seconds of silence following his offer, "what do you say?"

"I'd like to ask a few questions," Tom replied.

"That's only fair," conceded Mr. X. "We'll not promise to answer anything you want to know, however," he stipulated.

"I think you'll answer this one," said Tom,

with a smile. "There are always two sides to
an offer," he went on. "One is money, or some
other payment. You have that on your side.
Now what am I to give in exchange for this million dollars? That's a fair question, isn't it?"

"Very much so," agreed Mr. X. "And a natural one. In exchange for the million we will
agree to give you, you, on your part, will hand
over to us all patent and other papers, including
sketches, designs, patterns and blue prints of
your so-called talking-picture machine. In
short, you will turn the complete invention over
to us, and further make a promise."

"What sort of a promise?"

"A promise to go no farther in that field. In
other words, you will forget that such a machine
is capable of being made. You will wipe it out
of your mind after you have turned all your
rights in it over to us."

"And may I inquire what you will do with my
machine when you get it?" asked Tom, with a
curious smile as he shifted about in his chair, as
though it was no longer comfortable. "If you
do get it in exchange for a million dollars," he
added.

"We'll burn it up—destroy it!" excitedly cried
Mr. B.

Tom Swift could not help starting in surprise.
The answer was not quite what he had expected.

He looked for confirmation toward the masked Mr. X, thinking the big man might have spoken impulsively. But, somewhat to the astonishment of the young inventor, the leader nodded in assent.

"Once you turn your invention over to us in exchange for the million dollars," stated Mr. X, "it becomes our exclusive property for us to do with as we please. And, very likely, we shall destroy it."

"What for?" Tom could not help impulsively asking.

"To prevent our business from being ruined, young man! That's why!" burst out Mr. B. "Do you think," he went on in spite of the effort Mr. X made to silence him, "we want people to stay at home listening to music and seeing pictures of a performance on your screen? Where would we be if millions of people did about pictures what they are doing right now with their radio receivers? We'd be ruined in six months and we have millions tied up in our theaters— millions! No, sir. Once we get your machine we'll destroy it!"

"You haven't got it yet," Tom saw fit to remind him quietly. "And now, since you have been frank with me I will be the same with you. Your offer of a million dollars seems big to you. But let me tell you this. If you offered me ten

millions with the proviso that my machine be
destroyed I'd snap my fingers at you as I do
now!" and Tom suited the action to his words,
rising from the chair as he did so.

"Gentlemen, I shall bid you good evening!"
he went on. "I have found out what I wanted
to know."

Suddenly Mr. B's fingers went to the mask on
his face. Evidently he feared it had slipped and
revealed his identity. Tom could not help smiling as he said:

"Oh, I don't know who you are personally,
and I don't know that I care. It may make no
difference. But I can discover your identities
if I choose. That is neither here nor there.
The point is I refuse your offer and I'm going
back to my laboratory and perfect my machine.
Inside of a month it will be on the market!"

"Oh! oh!" wailed Mr. B. Some of the others
showed evidence of perturbation, but Mr. X remained calm.

"Sit down again, Mr. Swift," he said, and his
tone was not as smooth as before.

"Is that a command or an invitation?" asked
Tom sharply.

"You may regard it either way you like," was
the reply. And Tom did not need to be told
that the playing was over—stern reality was
now to the fore. The men still had masks on

their faces, but they no longer masked their intentions.

"Just a minute," said Tom, still standing by the chair. "You said, at the beginning that I was here of my own free will—that I could walk out of here any time I wished."

"That was true at the time it was stated," said Mr. X. "I may withdraw my offer any time."

"Have you withdrawn it?"

There was a moment's pause and then came the low reply:

"I have. Yes."

"Then I am not free to go?"

"Not until you listen further to me," said Mr. X. "I think you are very unwise, Tom Swift. We have made you a liberal offer. It is much more than you can make for a long time if you market your apparatus. We are interested in controlling it. What difference does it make to you whether we buy the machine and manufacture it in such quantities as we please or if we buy it and destroy it—as long as you get your price?"

"That's just it!" replied Tom angrily. "I'm not getting my price."

"We might increase our offer," suggested Mr. X.

"A certain man once said," remarked Tom

slowly, "that he was poor, but, poor as he was, the King of England was not rich enough to buy him. I say the same to you now. I am in need of funds—I do not hesitate to admit that. But, slender as my bank balance is, there is not enough cash among you masked men to pay me for destroying a machine I have worked so hard over—a machine which I hope will prove to be a delight to humanity. That's my answer. In other words, I defy you! I'm through! I'm going to walk out of here now. This conference is ended!"

"Oh, no, it isn't ended yet," said Mr. X in sinister tones as he arose and stepped toward a push button on the wall. "We have something else to say to you, Tom Swift. I didn't want to resort to harsh means, but there seems to be no hope for it."

"Wait a minute!" exclaimed the young inventor. "I think I understand your game. Perhaps you think you can torture me into giving in. Or you may even have it in mind to kill me, thinking, thereby, to prevent my machine from being perfected and going on the market.

"Listen to what I say. If you do away with me it will make no difference to that machine. It is complete and will be made and marketed. Full details of the invention are already in

Washington to be patented. More than this—
four models have been made. One is in my laboratory where you may get at it and destroy it
—I don't say you can't.

"But there are three other complete and working models in the hands of three friends of mine
in different parts of the country. They have
orders in case I do not reappear by a certain
time to make public all the facts and to put the
machine on the market."

"Oh! oh! He's got us beat!" lamented the
big man.

"No, he hasn't!" snarled Mr. X. "I'll force
him to do as we want him to."

"Oh, so you talk of force now, do you?" asked
Tom.

"Since you compel me—yes."

"Then it is time for me to play the same
game," went on the young inventor, with a tan-
talizing smile.

"What do you mean?" came from three of the
men, in evident alarm.

"My instructions were," said Tom, "to come
to this island alone. I did so, as you doubtless
know. But early this morning a number of my
friends preceded me here—and they are here
now. Gentlemen, this house is entirely surrounded. None of you can possibly escape—
neither you nor your Negro thugs. If I am not

permitted to walk out of here unmolested whenever I please, I will give the signal and you will at once be arrested."

"You think we will believe such a foolish statement as that?" scoffed Mr. X. "I tell you that you are at our mercy, Tom Swift! This house surrounded? Bosh!"

For answer Tom went to a window and raised the shade. At the same time he pressed the wall switch and plunged the room in darkness.

"Look!" cried Tom, and from the darkness outside, shining through the now dulled window glass, came a flashing light, thrice repeated.

There was a gasp of surprise from the masked men in the dark room.

"Look here!" went on Tom, moving to a window on the other side of the room. From the gloom without there shone another of the thrice flashing lights.

"It is the same on the other two sides of the house," remarked Tom.

The masked men sat silent, seemingly dazed.

"What is your answer now?" triumphantly asked the young inventor as it was made plain to the plotters that they were surrounded.

CHAPTER XXIII

TOM ACCEPTS

"GENTLEMEN," and Tom Swift put a peculiar emphasis on the word, "I repeat—what is your answer now?"

"Oh, the rascal! He's got us beat!" lamented the fat man. "Let's make terms with him."

"Make terms, nothing!" sneered Mr. X. "Those are nothing but lightning bugs! It's all a clever bluff!"

"Oh, is it?" asked Tom.

Again he stood in front of a window and, as he had done before, though unseen by the plotters, Tom raised and flashed the pocket electric torch he had brought with him. Once more, in answer to his signal, came more flashes from without. Tom's friends were on the alert.

"I guess that settles it," Mr. X was forced to admit. "Turn on the light here, Tom Swift, and we'll talk this matter over again."

"No!" exclaimed the young inventor in ringing tones. "I'll do the talking now—you'll do the listening. I'm in a position to dictate my terms, and I'll do it. I owe you something for the manner in which you had me and my manager kidnapped and brought to this place, also for what your tool Greenbaum did."

"Now listen here!" broke in Mr. B, his whole, fat body quivering with fear as Tom switched on the main light again. "That Greenbaum fellow, he went farther than we told him to. We never told him to try to blow you up, and we immediately discharged him when we learned of it."

"That is correct," assented Mr. X. "We do not countenance deeds of violence. Greenbaum, whom we have since discharged, went beyond his instructions—far beyond. But he was half crazy."

"Half crazy?" inquired Tom. "He always impressed me as being very level-headed—too much so."

"Still he was not right in his head," said Mr. B. "He lost a small fortune in a moving picture investment, and when he learned your invention might spell the ruin of that industry, so he could never recoup his losses, he went to desperate lengths."

"I should say he did," agreed Tom, with a grim smile, as he remembered his ruined laboratory and the pains he had suffered. "But I will exact payment for what he did."

"You would be within your rights there," said Mr. X.

"And for the indignities Mr. Newton and I suffered at the hands of Snogg, Janner and Torpy," went on the young inventor. "I suppose you will not deny that they acted for you?" he suggested.

"No, they were our agents," admitted Mr. B. "But we told them to treat you with respect, merely to hold you until we could get in touch with you. It was a mistake that Mr. Newton was kidnapped. We wanted you held. What terms do you offer?"

"I offer no terms at all. I demand unconditional surrender!" exclaimed Tom. "If you don't agree to that, I propose, to use a war term, to move immediately upon you. In other words, I'll give the signal for your arrest."

"Don't! Don't!" begged Mr. B shakingly.

"We are here to make terms, Mr. Swift," said a third masked man.

"What do you want us to do?" asked Mr. X, and there was no more threat or defiance in his voice. "You can name your own terms."

"In the first place," stipulated Tom, "I want you all to unmask. I don't care to do business with men I can't see. You might as well," he

added, as he saw them hesitate. "If you're arrested you will be known."

"Gentlemen, he is right!" said Mr. B. "Unmask!"

He set the example by doffing the black silk
that covered the upper part of his face. One
after another the five followed and Tom gasped
in surprise when he saw who the men were.
They were all important figures in the theatrical
and moving picture business.

"So that's the combination I've been up
against!" exclaimed the young inventor, as he
looked from one face to another. "I suppose I
should consider it quite an honor to have you
against me."

"In a way, yes," admitted the one still to be
designated as Mr. X. "You are a mighty lucky
and clever young man. Now we have met your
first stipulation, what is the next?"

"The next," stated Tom, "is that you must
sign a paper which I shall draw up, admitting
your share in all that has been done against me
and agreeing that all persecutions shall cease."

"Yes, that is no more than fair under the circumstances," agreed Mr. X.

"But you won't make that paper public—with
our names on it, will you?" asked Mr. B.

"Not if you let me entirely alone," promised
Tom. "But I want it to protect myself.

Hands off and that paper remains in my safe."

"Draw it up and we'll sign it," agreed Mr. X, after a hasty conference in one corner with his colleagues. "But what about the men you have posted out in the woods? Will they come in here and arrest us?"

"Not unless I give the signal," Tom answered. "It will not be given when you have signed that paper and I am allowed to walk out of here un‐ molested."

"Oh, let him go! Let him go!" begged Mr. B. "He'll have our watches and pocketbooks next! Let him go!"

Tom smiled grimly as he drew up the paper. He had the plotters entirely at his mercy. One after another they affixed their names to the document, and as he folded it and put it in his pocket, Mr. B said:

"Perhaps we can still talk business?"

"What do you mean?" asked Tom.

"Well, we made you an offer of a million dol‐ lars for the complete rights to your talking‐ picture invention that we might destroy it to save our business from ruin. You saw fit to decline that and you got the better of us in what followed. Now, since it seems that the inven‐ tion is going on the market, the next best thing for us to do is to buy into the exploiting com‐ pany and have a share in the profits. I suppose there will be profits?" he asked, with a somewhat quizzical smile. He was a big business man, as Tom knew.

"I hope there will be," Tom answered.

"Well, now that we've backed down—because you made us and for no other reason," went on Mr. B, "will you listen to another offer?"

"What is it?"

"We'll give you a million for a half share in the invention."

"Nothing doing!" exclaimed Tom, getting ready to leave.

"A million and a half!" offered Mr. B.

"Your figure is too low," replied Tom, who began to see daylight ahead for Ned Newton's financial embarrassment. "Why, you movie men put a million dollars in a single feature picture."

"Oh, quit being pikers!" put in another magnate. "Say two millions and be done with it! Come, what about two, young man?"

Tom made some rapid calculations. Two million dollars was a tempting offer for half an interest in the invention. He knew it would be on the market a long time before he would take in that much. Also he must have capital to manufacture the machines. But he still had a card to play.

"I can't accept that offer," he said, still moving toward the door.

"Oh, let's get this over with!" exclaimed Mr. X who, evidently, was used to having his own way. "We'll give you three millions for a half interest, Tom Swift, let you remain in virtual control, and we'll start manufacturing as soon as you demonstrate that it's a success. What do you say to that—three millions?"

"And that's our limit," put in another of the men, a tall, lean New Englander.

For a moment Tom Swift did not reply. To a casual observer it might have looked as though he was about to refuse that offer. He had made up his mind, but he did not want to seem too hasty. It was well that these men should know he was their master when it came to plotting and dickering.

"Well, how about it?" asked Mr. B anxiously. "Come, Mr. Tom Swift. Three millions aren't to be sneezed at."

"And I don't intend to sneeze!" said Tom suddenly, with a little chuckle. "Gentlemen, I accept your offer. Put it in writing and we'll call the conference over!"

CHAPTER XXIV

A FINAL TEST

THERE was a relieved air about the men gathered in the old house on Rattlesnake Island now that Tom Swift had made terms with them. Truth to tell, they had been more than a little afraid of this clear-eyed, keen young man who was able to dictate terms to them.

"Now let there be no mistake about this," said Tom. "We can draw up a new agreement, incorporating in it the terms of this one," and he produced the rough draft in which the men had agreed to molest him no longer.

"What do you want put in?" asked Mr. X, producing paper and a fountain pen.

"I want this three-million-dollar offer for a half interest in my invention put into an iron-clad agreement. I also want your written promise to interfere with me no longer."

"We aren't likely to bother you, considering that we are now associated with you in this thing," observed Mr. B.

"Well, it will do no harm to put it in," decided Tom. "Also, I want you to acknowledge full responsibility for the actions of your men, Greenbaum and the others, and your promise to send them far away from here."

"That's no more than fair," agreed Mr. X. "Those men went further than we told them to do. We had no sympathy with Greenbaum's attempt to blow you up and——"

"It was more than an attempt," interrupted Tom, with a grim smile. "There really was a disastrous explosion and I expect to be paid damages for that out of your share of the profits. I want that in the agreement, too."

"You shall have it," promised Mr. X, though some of his colleagues made rather wry faces at Tom's exaction of his "pound of flesh." But he was within his rights, and he knew it.

In a short time the agreement was drawn up and signed by all of them, and then Mr. X remarked:

"Of course this is contingent upon your invention being a success, Mr. Swift. Your broadcasting of songs and music must be clear, the images of the performers on the attached screen must be very plain, not shadowy forms, and the two must synchronize. You must remember that we have not seen your invention. All we know is what we have heard of it."

"From your spies, doubtless," Tom responded bitterly. "And they could find out very little. But don't worry. The machine must be perfect before I put it on the market. I am going to have a final test and you may witness it in person or you may send any one you like to report."

"Some of us will probably be on hand when you give a final showing," said Mr. X. "And now, as it is getting late, I suggest that we adjourn. We want to get back to our homes and you do also, I suppose, Mr. Swift?"

"Yes, I don't feel like spending another night on Rattlesnake Island," replied Tom, with a smile. "One was enough. I'll call in my friends and you can come to my final test—say a week from to-night in my private laboratory."

"Thank you," said Mr. X.

Tom bade the men good-night and went out into the darkness, leaving the conspirators to growl somewhat among themselves at having been beaten by a mere youth.

"At the same time," said Mr. X, "I can't help admiring Tom Swift for the manner in which he turned the tables on us."

"That's right," chimed in another. "He's the pluckiest fellow I ever had any dealings with. And to think, if we'd persisted, he could have had us all arrested and our names and our pictures would have been in the papers. Whew!"

"Oh my!" wailed Mr. B. "It's cost us a pretty penny, but maybe it will be worth it."

Meanwhile Tom, outside the old house, was signaling with his flashlight to call his friends in from their posts about the place.

"Is everything all right?" asked Ned, who led one of the four parties. He glided to his chum's side from the darkness.

"Everything is settled, and we get three million dollars for a half interest," said Tom, producing the agreement.

"Hot dog!" gleefully cried Ned. "That's the best news yet! We sure will need that money, Tom! I couldn't have held the banks off much longer. Good for you!"

In a short time Tom and Ned, with Mr. Damon, Koku and Eradicate were on their way back across Lake Carlopa, leaving the other members of the Swift party to follow in other boats as they pleased.

Though Tom Swift had gone to Rattlesnake Island alone as he had been bidden, the setting of his trap called for many of his most trusted men to precede him to the rendezvous. They had gone at intervals so no suspicions would be aroused.

So, during the day before the night of the meeting, several parties of seemingly innocent fishermen might have been seen landing on the island at a point farthest removed from the dock used by Tom. These parties were posted in the woods on four sides of the frame house and there they waited for Tom's signal. Ned was in charge of one party and Mr. Damon of another. Garret Jackson and his assistant took command of the two remaining squads.

"And bless my fountain pen!" exclaimed Mr. Damon as they were talking matters over on their way home in Tom's boat, "I thought you were never going to flash the signals, Tom."

"It took a little time to get things where I wanted them," the young inventor said. "But it worked out all right. They certainly were astonished."

"Do you think they'll play square with you, Tom?" asked Ned.

"They'll have to, for their own safety. I've got them where they can't help themselves. After the final demonstration, a week from to-night, we get the three millions."

"I suppose there is no doubt, Tom, as to the success of the thing?" ventured Ned.

"Not the slightest!" Tom's voice was full of confidence.

Grumblings and growlings were heard issuing from the throat of Koku. Tom asked what the trouble was.

"He's complaining because there was no

fight!" chuckled Mr. Damon. "He says Ned promised him that he could get hold of some of your enemies, Tom, but it all fizzled out."

"Me want smash um!" growled the giant, clenching his big fists.

"Too bad!" chuckled Tom. "But I couldn't pull off the fight, Koku. Better luck next time."

Tom made his motorboat fast to his own private dock and went home to tell his father the good news—that all matters were satisfactorily settled. He knew the aged inventor would be worried.

"I'm glad you're back, Tom," Mr. Swift said when he saw his son. "Now you can take it easy. You've been working too hard."

"The hard work isn't over yet," the young inventor answered. "I still have to give a perfect final test."

To this end he and Ned and the workmen bent all their energies during the next six days. Mr. Swift aided where he could and Mr. Damon was again called on to do his funny song and dance. Now that the invention was about to be made public and Tom had no fear about his patents being stolen from him, the affair could be openly talked about.

"Are you going to ask us to the dress rehearsal?" inquired Mary, when Tom was spending an evening with her.

"Better than that—I want you to be in it," he said.

"In it?"

"Yes, you and Helen. I want to see how ladies' garments will be shown on the screen. Ned and Mr. Damon balk at becoming female impersonators. Will you help?"

"Delighted! Oh, Tom, I do hope it will be a success!"

The night of the final test came at last. Several changes had been made both in the projecting machine and in the broadcasting studio since Tom's last attempt to show talking pictures. He had put a metallic curtain with reflecting mirrors in the room where Mr. Damon and Ned had done their part and the results were better.

"Though some day, Ned," Tom said to his chum, after a preliminary test, "I'll show these images without the use of any screen at all. I'll pick the electric impulses right out of the air just as wireless sound waves come now."

"That will mean you can broadcast from any theater without the use of this sort of curtain," Ned remarked, pointing to the one in the broadcasting room.

"That's right. All that will be needed in the theater will be a small cabinet, out of sight, on the stage.   But more of that later.   Now we'll go ahead with the test."

The moving picture and theatrical men, representing the syndicate that had bought a half interest in Tom's invention, were on hand in the studio.   They had brought with them some experts who were to pass on certain phases of the machine.   Mr. Damon, with Ned and the two girls were in the studio.   Tom Swift, with Mr. Jackson and some men to assist him, was busy at the projecting machine by means of which the audience hoped to hear the distant music and see the performers through several solid walls.

"All ready, Ned?" Tom asked over the private telephone.

"All set," was the answer.

"Then get going!" ordered Tom in a low voice.

He turned the switch for the final test, knowing that a great deal depended on it.   Those three million dollars were sorely needed to save the Swift fortunes.

CHAPTER XXV

A BRIGHT FUTURE

THERE was a hissing, buzzing sound in the studio where, on an improvised stage, Ned, Mr. Damon, Mary Nestor and Helen Morton were going through a hastily sketched act.

Tom Swift had so improved his lighting arrangements, by using screen filters, that there was no restriction as to the color of the garments worn by the performers. The girls' dresses were particularly gay and of many hues, for Tom wanted a bright picture on the screen. Mr. Damon had attired himself as a clown while Ned was a pirate with a red handkerchief on his head.

"Oh, a pirate's life for me!" sang Ned, and so on with the rest of the song while the girls and Mr. Damon joined in.

On his part, in the laboratory room, Tom had adjusted the switches and stood near his machine. Ranged in a semicircle in front of him was the audience.

"Everything is ready, gentlemen," said the

young inventor in a low voice. "You will now see and hear what I have to offer."

Suddenly, through the loud speaker, came the voices of the performers, as clear and distinct as though they were in the same room. There was no blasting effect, no tinny, horn-like element in the music.

A moment later the metallic glass screen attached to the apparatus glowed with a white light and before the eyes of the astonished gathering there appeared, in reduced form, but plainly and clearly, the images of the performers in a room several hundred feet away. Just as on a moving picture screen, only not as large, but beautifully colored and clearer than ever moving pictures had been, the images of Mary, Helen, Mr. Damon and Ned were observed. They smiled, gestured and went through various motions, not one of which was obscured and not one but synchronized exactly with the words they used.

"That's my invention," said Tom Swift simply. "If you think it is a success we can complete the deal."

"I guess there's no question of it," said Mr. X. "I, for one, am satisfied and as soon as——"

He ceased speaking, for suddenly, in the midst of a song by the performers in the studio, the voices died away and the images faded from the screen.

"Don't cut it off!" begged Mr. B.   "I was just beginning to enjoy it."

"I didn't cut it off!" Tom answered quickly. "There's something wrong!"

Then, from the corridor without, the voice of Koku was heard crying:

"I cotch him!   I got him!   Now I make him like jelly!"

Like an echo came a frightened voice begging:

"Let me go!   Oh, let me go!"

"Greenbaum!" shouted Tom, springing to the door in time to see the giant holding the plotting man in a grasp that made him helpless.

"I cotch him!" cried Koku.   "I be on watch out here like Mr. Tom always tell me.   I see him sneak along and cut wire.   He have big ball in his hand, too, but I knock it down. Over there in corner!"

Garret Jackson made a jump for the corner indicated and picked up something which made him utter an exclamation of dismay.

"It's a bomb!" the superintendent shouted.

There was a pail of water near by and into that the infernal machine was dropped just in time, for the fuse was spluttering and burning down.

Greenbaum, choked into senselessness by Koku's powerful grip, sank to the floor. Tom turned to the assembled moving picture and theater men. There was an implied accusation in his glance.

"I hope you will believe us when I say we had absolutely nothing to do with this," said Mr. X. "We have not seen Greenbaum since his former unauthorized attack on you. This is a terrible surprise to us."

"And to me, also," said Tom. "I don't know what damage he has done, but——"

"He not do much!" chuckled Koku. "Me cotch him in time."

And so it proved. Greenbaum had managed to sneak into the laboratory because vigilance was somewhat relaxed, now that all danger seemed over. He had cut one of the electrical wires that carried power to Tom's machine, hoping, in the confusion he knew would follow, to be able to plant his infernal machine and get away. But the giant was too quick for him.

"Is the machine ruined?" asked Ned, coming from the broadcasting studio, followed by the other performers.

"Bless my apple pie! And just when I was going to sing my song!" complained Mr. Damon.

But a quick examination showed nothing more wrong than a severed wire, which was soon spliced, so that the machine could work again, and after Greenbaum had been handed over to the police, first needing the attention of a doctor, however, the interrupted performance went on to a successful conclusion.

When the little playlet was ended, and the men engaged by Mr. X and his colleagues had made their report, the leader of the theatrical interests announced:

"We are satisfied, Mr. Swift. The deal can go through. You will be paid the three million to-morrow and we will at once form a company for manufacturing these machines and put them on the market. But I am afraid you still feel that we sent Greenbaum here."

"No," Tom answered, "I have good reasons for knowing you did not."

"What reasons?" asked Mr. X in surprise.

"Because the man is insane. The doctor told me so just before he was taken away. You told me his losses in a moving picture deal had so turned his brain that he did more than you wanted him to when you first set him to spy on me. Well, his insanity is of a progressive form, and he is much worse now. He probably imagined that I was the cause of all his troubles, and so came to be revenged on me. I know you had nothing to do with it."

"I am glad you are convinced of that," said

Mr. X. "And we have to thank you for treating us even better than, perhaps, we deserved. But from now on we will work in harmony."

This promise was faithfully kept. Much to Ned Newton's relief the sum of three millions was placed to the credit of the Swift concern the next day, and certain maturing notes were taken up. There was a goodly capital left, however, to start the manufacture of the talking-picture machines and they were soon put on the market, meeting with a big success. The radio and moving picture people, as well as several big theatrical interests, bought stock in the new company that was formed, and because of Tom's invention, by means of which only authorized purchasers of his machine could view the broadcast scenes and listen to the music, there was no "bootlegging," which meant that all the revenues would come to those entitled to them.

Tom was glad to learn, later, that Greenbaum's insanity was not permanent, and that after the man was assured of a chance to make another fortune in the new business, his mind became calm and he was himself again. He was totally unaware of the outrages he had committed, though when told of them asked Tom's forgiveness.

Snogg, Janner and Torpy were not heard of

again, and the house on Rattlesnake Island, which was the property of the moving picture men, was made over to Tom as a sort of bonus. He and Ned spent many hours there, relaxing from their hard work

It was after Greenbaum's recovery, when certain things were recalled to him, that he explained what for a time had puzzled Ned and Tom. The man, who was an expert electrician, had found a means of neutralizing certain parts of the electrified fence. Hence he was able to get over, after the discovery of the planted bombs, to commit petty depredations that so annoyed Tom.

It was Greenbaum, also, who provided the fash melon that had thrown Koku off his guard. As Tom had guessed, the fruit was discovered in South America by a party of travelogue movie men who brought some back with them. Greenbaum, learning of Koku's fondness for fash, used it to play what was nearly a fatal trick on the giant. Greenbaum had also been responsible for the "warning" Eradicate brought to Tom. That was just a bluff—intended to scare Tom, but it worked the other way.

The secret passage in the house on Rattlesnake Island was easily accounted for. The place had been built some years before to be used in making a certain moving picture, where a secret staircase played a part. Later the house was acquired by Mr. X and his colleagues to use as a prison and also as a meeting place for Tom.

Tom suitably rewarded Bill Tagg, the tramp, and that individual had his long ardent wish fulfilled. He rode in one of Tom's aeroplanes and received the thrill of his life.

"Well, everything came out all right, didn't it?" asked Ned of his chum as they sat in the house on Rattlesnake Island one evening after a successful day's fishing. "Your talking pictures are making a hit."

"They seem to be," admitted Tom modestly. "Though when Greenbaum cut the wire that night of the final test I thought everything had gone bad. But, as you say, everything came out all right, and the future looks rosy to me. I've got another scheme in my mind."

"Aren't you ever going to stop?" chuckled Ned as he leaned lazily back in his chair.

"Not as long as I feel as well as I do now," replied Tom Swift.

Whether he carried out his new idea or not remains to be seen.

THE END